Murder on the Court

THE UNSCRIPTED DETECTIVE
BOOK 2

BARBARA BARRETT

Paperback ISBN: 978-1-948532-77-8

This book is dedicated to teams. Those who work together, those who play together and people who find themselves grouped together for whatever the reason. When everyone knows and follows through on their responsibilities, teams tend to work. When that isn't the case, for whatever reason, teams don't function well.

This is the story of a pickleball team and a work team that fall in that second group. In large part, they are dysfunctional due to an overbearing, egocentric coach and boss. When she pushes one of them too far, they kill her. In the aftermath, is there hope the team can heal and move forward?

one

. . .

*K*eep *putting one foot in front of the other,* temporarily grounded TV star Marla Dane told herself in order to stay focused on her exercise routine. There might not be any acting gigs on the horizon, but she'd been in the business long enough to know she had to keep mind and body ready for the day that golden opportunity presented itself. Especially when that mind was in its mid-sixties and the body five-eight.

She'd forgotten that mantra after months had gone by without being offered any parts. After she'd trusted a compadre with financing for a project she could barely afford, only to see nothing materialize. After she'd spent months holed up in her Brentwood, California home not socializing, too humiliated to be seen. After she'd returned to her home state of Minnesota to stay with her sister and regroup, only to be engulfed in solving a murder that occurred on her doorstep.

But now she was back on track. And not just the one on this treadmill. On reflection, it was hard to believe a fictional TV PI could actually help uncover a real-life killer. Still, she'd pulled it off. But not without the support of her sister, Kitty Lovejoy;

the local police chief and his wife; and Rex Alcorn, retired St. Paul, Minnesota, cop and fellow resident in her sister's condo building. There'd been no script, just her own intuition, intelligence and a few memories of her alter ego from *Carruthers on the Case*, Letitia Carruthers, to guide her. Oh, and Rex's sardonic advice.

Go figure. Her golden opportunity back in LA was still in the future, but the old Marla Dane, the self-confident woman with slightly graying red hair, had begun to reemerge. Even her blue-green eyes had regained most of their sparkle. And this Marla Dane knew as much as she hated exercise, she and this treadmill in the condo building's fitness room were fated to be everyday companions.

Her late husband, Carson Grant, had installed a fitness room in their home years ago when she got her first starring role in a film so she could stay in shape. He didn't like the idea of her fighting LA traffic even for the two-mile drive to the closest workout center. The room was set up just for her preferred machines and was located just off the shower/dressing room and near the entrance to the pool.

The equipment was more limited in this condo fitness room, but she only used the treadmill and stationary bike anyhow. The constant blowers kept her cool, and the air filtration system allowed her to breathe air that wasn't cloying as it disguised the odor of sweating bodies. And she'd learned if she hit it around ten in the morning, she could have peace and quiet.

"Wouldn't you rather get your exercise out in the fresh air?" a woman's voice asked from behind her.

The voice belonged to Scottie Richards, another condo resident. Scottie had been the first to welcome Marla to Rambling Meadows Condominiums when she arrived a few weeks earlier. Locked out in the middle of a sudden rainstorm because Kitty had failed to pick her up at the airport, Marla had been a wet mess. Scottie had taken pity on her and admitted her to the secure building.

Marla kept up her measured pace on the treadmill. "I like it here. It's private."

"You, the successful TV star? I thought you thrived on having an audience," Scottie said, sliding around to the front of the machine to be in Marla's view, her off-to-the-side gray bangs a front drape today. Like Marla, she was in her mid-sixties.

"Not so much since I left the show." She hoped her visitor would get the message and leave. Not that she had anything against the woman. Scottie had prevailed upon Rex Alcorn to let her into Kitty's condo that fateful day of her arrival.

"Are you sure you want this much privacy?" Scottie pursued.

Why was Scottie so interested in how she was getting her exercise? There was more to this than just friendly concern. "Why are you really here, Scottie?"

Scottie's lips folded in briefly before replying. "You saw through me. How 'bout you turn off this contraption long enough for me to make my pitch?"

At least she was willing to drop the pretense of being interested in her well-being. Marla hit the Stop button and waited for the belt to do the same. "Okay. Better?" She gripped each of the machine's arms and leaned in. "What do you really want?"

Scottie released a breath before proceeding. "I need a teensy-weensy favor."

"If I learned anything from my years in Hollywood, it's never trust someone who says *teensy-weensy*."

Scottie had the grace to make a face. "Sorry. Not the best way to start. I'll try again."

"Make it good. I still have ten minutes of my routine to go."

"I have a chance to attend the Taylor Swift concert in Chicago this coming weekend. I apparently made a commitment to Eloise Wallace, the owner of a local PR firm, a few weeks back that I'd forgotten about. I need someone to substitute for me this Saturday so I can go. That would be you."

Scottie had neglected to say what she needed a substitute for. That omission couldn't be good. "Substitute for what?"

"You played tennis out in California, right? Everyone out there plays tennis."

"You want me to play tennis for you?" It had been years since she'd walked on a court. Why would this woman think she could possibly play the game now? She must be really desperate.

"Actually, this is a newer version of the game. Less strenuous, especially for those of us on the other side of fifty. Ever heard of pickleball?"

Pickleball? That's what this was about? "In passing. It's been in vogue in California a few years, although until recently I was always too busy to try it myself." She didn't mention that she would've had the time more recently since being let go by the producers of *Carruthers on the Case*.

Scottie took another big breath. "I need you to step in for me at my pickleball game this Saturday."

"*Step in*, as in play in your place?" Surely she wasn't serious.

"Play? No. I couldn't expect you to learn how to play in just a few days. My job is to provide water to anyone who wants it."

"You want me to be water girl?" Marla didn't bother to disguise her repulsion.

"I prefer to call myself Hydration Manager," Scottie replied.

Marla restrained the belly laugh she'd been about to unleash at the thought of someone calling herself a hydration manager. Scottie was serious about this. "Don't most people have their own fancy water bottles these days?" she asked. "Why can't the team members depend on those for *hydration*?"

"They can and they do. In fact, I don't get called upon to give out water very often. But apparently some of the larger, better-funded teams bring their own water person. Eloise pays attention to appearances, so she insists her team have one too."

Marla stared her down. "You may have been conned by Drake Elliot initially, but you saw through him and called things off before giving him any money. How does someone so smart and self-assured agree to give up her Saturdays just to give out water?"

Scottie rubbed the back of her neck before replying. Looking for a way to justify her action? "Now I see why you were able to catch Elliot's killer. You see through people and persist in questioning them until you get an answer."

"Just answer my question."

"I want to go back to work. I'm fixed financially, but I need something to keep me busy. Clubs and charities are fine but not fulfilling. I've watched how you've bounced back from a terrible setback in your life out on the West Coast by helping the police. I don't have that kind of chutzpah, but I am creative and clever. I thought PR might be my bag. Even if on a part-time basis."

Marla fought to keep up. "How does handing out water relate to PR?"

"Eloise told me she'd consider bringing me in on a consulting capacity if I'd do this favor for her."

Who was this Eloise? Her arrangement with Scottie seemed kind of one-sided to her. But that was for Scottie to decide. "How long does this favor last?" she asked instead.

"In your case, just this coming weekend," Scottie replied. "For me, the rest of the season, I guess."

Good thing winter wasn't that far off. Did they play pickleball off-season?

"You'll need to get the water on your own, but the team will reimburse you afterwards," Scottie said.

"Bottled water?"

Scottie chuckled, seemingly amused by Marla's hesitation.

"You like specifics, don't you? Yes, bottled water. Chill it before-hand. Two or three large bottles should do it."

"Where do I take all this?" Marla asked.

"The court, of course. It's part of the Rambling Meadows complex behind our building."

"Okay. I haven't gotten over there yet. But I'm sure I can find it. What time?"

"Ten in the morning. Should take a few hours. So? You'll do it?"

"Just this once, right?" Marla said firmly, only willing to commit to one week. At least until she got a better idea about this pickleball.

"Right."

"Okay. One time. This Saturday."

A gleeful Scottie clapped her hands. "Terrific! Thank you, thank you, thank you. I owe you one."

She was gone before Marla could think further about what she had agreed to.

SHOWERED, with the day's stint on the treadmill completed, Marla settled herself in front of her notepad computer at Kitty's kitchen island. Even though Kitty told her to use the desk in her study anytime she wanted, Marla had gravitated to this spot whenever she needed to check something online. It might be less private, but it was also less formal. She didn't mind Kitty looking over her shoulder occasionally, unless she was checking out entertainment news.

Right now, she needed to learn all she could about pickleball before Saturday so she could give the appearance she had some idea what was going on. Old habit when taking on a new role or when *Carruthers on the Case* involved an unfamiliar angle.

Pickleball apparently was similar to tennis in that it involved serving with a paddle, albeit one different from a regulation tennis racket. Players hit a ball that was slightly different from a tennis ball, more like a Wiffle ball, over a net that ran between the two sides of the court. Besides the rackets and balls, it differed in that the ball had to bounce twice, once on each side, before it could be volleyed back and forth. There was also a "no-bounce" area seven feet from the net on each side. This was referred to as the *kitchen*. The ball could not bounce there or it ended the volley. Another contrast: The serve was underhanded as compared with the overhand serve in tennis.

Sounded like an interesting game, although there was no way she'd ever play. Even though it was gaining a lot of popularity with seniors, this sixty-something senior was content to limit her participation in the sport to being Water Girl. Or Hydration Manager, to borrow from Scottie.

She'd agreed to do something she had no idea how to handle. Like when did she show up? Who was her team? Who did she report to? Was there a captain? Or did they call whoever was in charge something else?

Why hadn't she thought of these questions when Scottie was still in begging mode, when she would've been ready to take whatever time was needed to fill Marla in?

"Why is your face screwed up like that?" Kitty asked from where she lounged against the kitchen doorframe.

"I agreed to be the substitute water person at a pickleball game this weekend, and I have no idea what pickleball entails. I'm surprised Scottie didn't ask you first." Then it hit her. "She did, didn't she? And you must've turned her down. How? Did you invent some reason, or is your dance card already full on Saturday morning?"

Kitty didn't reply right away. Instead, she stuck her head in the fridge and emerged with a yogurt cup. "Is that what she was hinting around about? She never did tell me what she wanted because I told her I was judging a pie-baking contest on Saturday."

This was news. But then, Kitty's schedule was more complicated than the president's. "Don't take this personally, but are you even qualified to judge someone's skill at pie baking?"

Kitty raised her brows. "How could I not take that personally? Are you implying my knowledge of pie baking is not what it should be to judge someone else's pies?"

"As far as I know, your pie-baking skills suck."

"Don't worry about hurting my feelings," Kitty replied.

"But I'm right, though, aren't I? How did you get recruited for this job?"

Kitty swept a hand through her shoulder-length locks. "I was asked."

"Really? By whom?"

Her sister drew up her shoulders, her go-to mode for defensiveness. "I'm offended you'd even question how I got involved."

"You're also not answering. Spill."

Kitty pouted briefly. "Hub Sherman is the local marketing VP for Prairie Harvest Flour. He dreamed up this contest to gain more attention for his product. He needed volunteers and turned to me."

"Hub Sherman? That's a new name for me. I don't suppose you're seeing him socially?"

"Why do you jump to that conclusion anytime I mention a man's name?"

"Because it usually means you are."

Kitty sniffed. "Just a lucky guess. I happened to meet him at a cocktail party hosted by Delphine Rambling last week."

"Rambling as in Rambling Meadows Condominiums?" Marla asked. How did Kitty know the bigwigs who had developed this property on the family farm a few years back?

"Right. Can you believe it? And for once it wasn't because she wanted to meet my celebrity sister. At least your name never came up when we talked. Then."

Marla had been so pleased for her sister until that last word. "Then? That means I was mentioned at another time. What did you commit me to?"

Kitty brought her yogurt over to the island and planted herself in a chair next to Marla. "I did something I hope you'll interpret as my protecting your privacy. Apparently word has gotten around that you are living here in this building. Delphine, who's the honorary chair of this pie-baking event, tried to get hold of you, but no one had your number or email. She got resourceful and called me."

"That's when she invited you to her party?"

"I explained that you were keeping a low profile while you're visiting and I suspected you'd turn her down. Some might have said thank you and left it at that, but she was gracious enough to invite me, since the subject had already been raised."

Marla had to laugh. Instead of trying on the few pieces in her big sister's wardrobe that had come from *Carruthers* even though she was two inches shorter than Marla's five foot eight, now Kitty was stepping in socially for her. But that was okay. Kitty might as well benefit from what remained of Marla's fame. "And you don't mind acting as my stand-in?"

Kitty's eyes fluttered momentarily, like her brain was shifting into gear. "When it gained me entrée to the famous Rambling Mansion? No. Plus I met Hub that way." A few beats went by while Kitty must be considering her next words. "You don't mind, do you? I was going to tell you. Really. I, uh, was waiting for the right time."

"Which is now, since I called you out on it." Marla offered Kitty a loving, sisterly smile so Kitty would know she wasn't upset with her. She was aware that Kitty had at times traded on

Marla's name, but that had been before Marla arrived in town, and, from as much as Marla knew, simply to impress her friends. Accepting an invite in lieu of Marla was a step up. Marla wasn't concerned, but she did file the scenario away in her head.

Although people here in Minnesota were aware she'd been let go from the show, they weren't aware of the extent of her depression resulting from the lack of new projects. Her celebrity was still viable, meaning she and Kitty needed to have a serious discussion, soon, about the degree to which Kitty could trade on it.

two

. . .

"Scottie suggested I take two or three large bottles of water. How am I supposed to transport them there?" Marla asked Kitty once she'd finished her yogurt.

Kitty nodded, now understanding. "How about I help you if you help me first?"

"Always the negotiator. What do you need from me?"

"Even though you've become a big television star, before that, before you left for Broadway, you were a pretty good baker. Chocolate chip cookies, especially, but you could also make a mean pie crust. Teach me how to do the same."

Her sister's request surprised her. "I thought you said you were asked to judge the pie baking, not make one yourself."

"I was and I will, but I have no idea what to judge. I thought if I witnessed the entire process beforehand, I might have a fighting chance knowing what to evaluate."

Marla tried to recall the last time she'd baked a pie but couldn't. Perhaps in an attempt to impress her new husband when she and Carson were first married? Otherwise, her last pie had to have been produced while she was still living at home here in Minnesota with their parents.

"I'd like to help you, Kitty, but it's been years since I've baked a pie. I'm afraid I'd spend so much time trying to recall Grandma's crust recipe, my process wouldn't be at all helpful."

"I'll even go with you to the grocery store to pick up the ingredients."

"Thanks, but having the right ingredients is just the beginning. I have no idea what happened to my old recipe. I got so busy with my acting career shortly after Carson and I were together, we hired a housekeeper who prepared our meals, and I stopped cooking and baking."

"No problem. I'll go online and find several for you to choose from," Kitty said.

"Isn't there someone else in the building you could ask for help? Maybe Kaitlin Fargo or Rita Haley? They owe us for clearing their names in the Elliot murder."

"They're appreciative and relieved that you and Rex Alcorn discovered the real killer, but they're also still waiting to get the money back that they invested with that scam artist."

"Surely they don't hold Rex and me accountable for the amount of time it's taking to work through all the red tape involved with the restitution process?" Both women had been foolish enough to give the late con man several thousand dollars of their money. She and Rex had discovered the numbers, which a state code breaker had tracked down to the right account. But until the two victims got their money back, they weren't completely satisfied.

"Forget about them. Why should I look elsewhere when I've got the real deal living here in my condo?" Another thought occurred to her. "Besides, other than lying around all day, what have you been doing since you solved that murder?"

Now she was playing dirty. Kitty had been the one to urge Marla to take it easy for a bit while she came down from the high level of tension she'd experienced facing a killer. "It just looks like I've been lazing around. My body and mind and spirit have been regrouping."

"Fine. Using your hands to roll out a crust and preparing the filling will be great therapy."

Kitty wasn't about to drop this idea. There was no recourse but to give in, but Marla wanted to get something out of it for herself besides recharging her culinary skills. "This needs to be a fair exchange. Suggesting how I lug that water to the court doesn't stack up against baking a pie, especially when I haven't made one in years."

Kitty opened her mouth to protest but immediately closed it. "What would you consider a *fair exchange*?"

That was a stumper. Why had she even mentioned it? What favor could Kitty do for her? What she needed most was a new part. Kitty couldn't help her there.

Before Marla could think of something, Kitty came up with an idea of her own. "Why don't you do your own podcast?"

"Me? Do a podcast?"

"It's a perfect idea, despite the fact that it was Rex who first suggested it when you were investigating the murder. It would be something to fill your time while you're reevaluating your career."

Although she didn't exactly reject the idea, Marla couldn't see how it would fit into her current state of unemployment. "What would I do in a podcast?"

Kitty shrugged. "That's up to you, but think about it. It'd be one way you could keep your name in front of the public while you're waiting for a new project to come along. If it generated enough subscribers, you might even earn a few bucks."

"Perhaps I could use it as a vehicle to showcase my acting chops?"

"I guess. It would have to be your speaking chops, though. Podcasts are about audio."

"Audio? I was thinking more about being seen. Isn't there some way to do that?"

Kitty considered. "Yes, although my knowledge of that technology is even more limited than it is with podcasts. Are you familiar with YouTube? It's one of the best known sources of videocasting. There are others. I'm just not familiar with them. If that's the direction you want to go, do some Internet research. Or talk to Rex. From what Tom Casey has told me, he and Rex have been playing around with producing their own video."

"Rex doing his own video? That doesn't sound like him," Marla replied. Did she really want to ask Rex for help so soon after he'd helped her with the investigation? He hadn't been particularly excited about working with her at first, although by the time they were confronting the killer together, they'd developed a certain working relationship.

"I think I recall Tom telling me he would be the one in front of the camera and Rex would be behind the scenes. Tom told me Rex was helping him get started. Since you made that face when I mentioned Rex, maybe you could ask Tom for help instead."

"I still don't know what I'd do in a podcast or a ... a ... what did you call it? Videocasting?"

Kitty's eyes brightened. "You could do one on baking an apple pie. Kill two birds with one pie, so to speak; demonstrate pie baking to me on video."

Kitty's mind was still on her own situation even though she was attempting to make it sound like she was helping Marla.

Tom Casey had been the one who finally got Marla to come back to Minnesota. Kitty had given up asking her to return after Marla spent several months feeling sorry for herself following being let go from *Carruthers*. To get her to return, Tom told her Kitty had been acting so erratic she needed her sister to get her back on course. As it turned out, that had been a ruse worked out between Kitty and Tom when

Kitty decided her invitation alone wouldn't bring her sister home.

Tom Casey also had a tough case of unrequited love for Kitty. He'd more or less admitted as much to Marla when she first arrived, but unlike every other man with whom Kitty came in contact, he wasn't about to put himself on the line and show her how much he cared.

"Tom Casey doesn't strike me as the type who puts himself out there on a video." What little contact she'd had with the man suggested the shy, comfy teddy bear type.

"It surprised me, too, when I learned he'd been investing in video equipment. So far, he's been supporting others' attempts to produce their own videos," Kitty said. "I'm not sure he'll ever do his own. Tom seems to be one of those people who drift from one idea to another."

Interesting observation from one who appeared to be doing the same. On the other hand, maybe it took one to recognize one. Like Kitty, Tom might be trying to "find" himself. Not the self-discovery sort of thing they'd gone through in their middle years but a new, senior form of it. In truth, she was probably going through her own version as she struggled to adapt to her newfound freedom.

"Okay," she said before she let herself think too much about all the drawbacks of doing a video. Although she wasn't familiar with how either of these media worked, she'd heard that many celebrities had turned to them as a way of staying in touch with their audiences.

Maybe she could do something that touched a bit on her private life without getting too "private." Even though it had been eons since she'd baked an apple pie, wouldn't it be like riding a bike after several years, something your brain and muscles remembered without much effort?

"Okay, let's try it. See if Tom's available tomorrow. Today I want to bake a test pie minus the camera and mic, just to be sure it all comes back to me."

"Next, we, uh ..." Marla had just combined the requisite amount of flour and salt in a medium-size bowl, and suddenly she couldn't remember what came next. "I'm sorry, Tom. Can you pause things while I check my recipe?"

"Sure, Marla," Tom Casey replied, his large brown eyes friendly and helpful. Such a puppy dog, with his graying ginger hair in need of a trim. "But just remember," he continued, "once you're doing this for real, it'll work best if you just keep going. We can always stop and edit later, but you run the risk of losing the spontaneity of the shoot if you keep stopping. Which is what is so appealing about videocasting."

What was wrong with her? Yesterday afternoon, even with Kitty sitting across from her taking notes, she'd made the crust and then the filling almost flawlessly. She'd only stopped once when some of the filling missed the pie plate and landed on the floor. Now, she couldn't even remember what went into the crust.

She was used to working in front of cameras. Several at the same time. Why was Tom's one camera causing her to forget what she was doing?

They tried it again, picking up where she'd left off once she'd consulted the recipe. The next item was the shortening. Her grandmother had taught her and Kitty to use solid shortening. Times had changed, and the type of shortening she'd selected now contained less trans fat in its makeup. Though the pie she'd made the day before had been tasty, with even Kitty approving of it, it still didn't taste quite the same as Grandma's pie crusts. Was that the different formula or just the fact she was no longer a kid, more easily impressed with her elder's cooking? Was that what was making her focus off-kilter?

Whatever the reason, the shortening was not blending with the flour combination the way it should. Tom had told her to keep going, but it was making her crazy that she couldn't get the flour and shortening to combine into the little pea-size shapes she was expecting.

After they'd stopped four more times, Tom called a break.

"I'm sorry, Tom. This didn't happen yesterday, and I've gone about this today exactly like I did then."

"You were doing it for yourself yesterday," Tom said helpfully. "Today you're too much aware of the camera. It seems to be affecting your rhythm."

"That's just the thing. I'm used to performing for the camera. And for an audience, with the production crew and other actors watching. I've never felt this tense before."

Tom drew in his lips, apparently at a loss how else to help.

"Why don't we take a fifteen-minute break and start over?" Kitty said. Remarkably, she'd been quiet all this time, remaining in the background behind Tom. "All new ingredients."

Marla wasn't convinced either the break or starting over would save this video, but she agreed to give it a try.

She left Tom and Kitty to discuss how to fix things while she went to her room and crashed, after putting a cold compress on her forehead.

The second try went a little better, but this time she messed up on the filling, completely forgetting to add the cinnamon and nutmeg.

"Just keep going," Tom said after she'd stopped. "Your audience will never know the final product is missing anything, especially since you'll run through the ingredients one last time at the end."

She'd compensated for forgotten lines and missed cues

many a time in the past. She'd also improvised when things didn't go exactly as planned. But today? Today was different. Her brain had fixated on the missing spices to the point of making her trip over later steps in the process.

Marla was a trouper. "The show must go on" was imprinted in her brain. But she knew when she finished how badly it had gone.

"Thanks for doing this today, Tom," she'd told him as he packed up his equipment. "You could've walked at any time, and I would've understood, but you hung in and got me to the end."

"I wish I knew how to help you past whatever seemed to be on your mind today," he replied. "You're a great actress, and that essence was coming through despite your other difficulties. Why don't we try this again in another week?"

"Thanks for the offer, but I don't think this is my path."

"Don't give up yet. Let me know when you want to resume, and I'll be there."

"Poor Tom," Kitty said after he left. "He thinks he let you down because he's not a professional director."

"Did he tell you that?" It was bad enough Marla had let herself down, but the thought that she'd had that effect on Tom was unbearable.

"No. He just takes things on himself sometimes when he shouldn't. Don't worry. I'll talk to him tomorrow and reassure him it wasn't his fault."

"Maybe I should be doing the reassuring?" Marla said.

"You've got enough on your mind."

"I was that bad?"

"You weren't bad, sis. You just didn't seem to click today."

"I appreciate your soft-pedaling my performance, but I think I'll write off doing my own video. It could've been a brand-new start for me, but I got in my own way."

"Don't be so hard on yourself. You took a chance. I still think you'd be great at it, once you get past your own mind."

And there was the rub. Marla agreed. Deep down she knew she would be great at this new medium, but something was keeping her from stepping up to the plate and hitting the home run she knew she could pull off. Did that something lie back in California and broken promises and dreams she'd run away from, or was there something new plaguing her since she'd come back to Minnesota? This mystery seemed even more insurmountable than investigating the death of a con man.

three

. . .

With her failure at creating her own video behind her, Marla threw her efforts into preparing to be Water Girl on Saturday. Kitty had come through on her promise to help her figure out how to get the water to the pickleball court by producing a service wagon and cooler from her storage unit in the underground parking garage.

"The only question remaining," she said to Kitty the night before the game, "is what I'm supposed to wear."

"Something comfortable," Kitty replied.

"What are the team's colors? I'll find something to match."

"Can't help you there. I've never been to one of their games."

That didn't surprise her. Unless there was an attractive male on an athletic team, Kitty didn't attend sporting events. "I wish I'd thought to ask Scottie when I agreed to step in for her. She's probably headed to Chicago already."

"Text her," Kitty said. "I've got her number if you don't have it."

An hour later, they had their answer. Olive green and white, plus the warning not to wear yellow as it drew players' attention away from the balls, most of which were yellow.

"Ooh, olive green is so not your color," Kitty said. "Not with your fair skin and graying red hair. Speaking of which, why haven't you done something about coloring it?"

"Good question. Guess I haven't had time to consider it since I arrived. I sort of cut back on that type of luxury in recent months. I no longer had the services of the show's hairdresser, and I didn't feel I could afford that level of expertise on my own dollar."

They'd been staring at the contents of Marla's closet. Kitty pulled her over to the bed and sat down beside her. "Speaking of which, we haven't talked about your finances since you've been here. I've sensed there was more to that story but left it to you to bring up. But since you did ..."

"I'm not destitute. The show gave me a decent payout, since I still had a year left on my contract. Plus, Carson and I established a sizable nest egg over the years, what with the properties he'd acquired before our marriage and the income from his screenwriting and my acting gigs once we were together. But for the first time in six years, I had to face the expenses the show had been covering, things like my transportation, meals, and my hair and makeup. That payout can only go so far."

"Oh, Marla! I didn't realize. I've always pictured you as richer than King Midas." She paused, apparently thinking through the implications of her sister's admission. "Did you have to sell your house? Is that why you finally decided to come here?"

Marla gave a half laugh. She didn't want to scare Kitty nor paint the situation worse than it was. And she still hadn't given her the full story behind her financial crisis. "No. I'm keeping my home in Brentwood and all my other properties except the mountain cabin I inherited from Carson. He went there to write. I never go there."

She didn't add that she'd used the proceeds from selling the cabin to invest in a project that had yet to see the light of day.

The producer friend to whom she'd given the money had assured her when they first talked that it was ready to launch as soon as he got the additional funding. She'd neglected the advice of her financial advisor to never invest in her own projects, to let the speculators absorb the cost, and she'd relearned why that made sense.

"You know you're welcome to stay with me as long as you like. This condo is paid off, and I just have minor living expenses."

"Thanks. For now, I'm accepting your offer, although I can more than cover your living expenses and mine. I mainly need a place where I can contemplate where I go from here. Somewhere that's comfortable and welcoming. And living here with you fits the bill exactly."

SATURDAY MORNING WAS one of those gifts to the Northland, when even though it was late fall, the temps were in the low seventies, the humidity nonexistent and the sky a brilliant blue. As much as she loved the warmth and perpetual green of California, her home state wasn't so bad either, especially if you preferred four seasons to one. In fact, if it wasn't for the mind-numbing cold of winter and the onset of healthier-than-they-deserved-to-be-mosquitoes—often referred to as the state bird—this was a real paradise.

The pickleball courts were part of a small recreational area for the use and enjoyment of the condo residents located behind the condo complex. The oasis was surrounded by a stand of maple, oak and fir trees. Four pickleball courts framed with a twenty-foot-high fence occupied a large sector of the interior. Four picnic tables, a charcoal grill and two wrought-iron benches sat off to the other side.

Marla hadn't been here before, but seeing the amenities now as she pulled the wagon behind her, she resolved to return another time when no pickleball games were underway. She could picture herself reading on one of those benches.

Six players were already setting up at various spots on one side of the net inside the fences.

"You're late for practice," a woman's accusatory voice said from behind her.

Marla turned to face the voice. It belonged to a heavily made-up woman in her forties or fifties, her graying dark hair pulled into a high ponytail, a pair of goggles with olive-green frames on her head.

"I'm not here for practice. I'm subbing for Scottie Richards today. I'm Mar—"

"Okay, fine. We don't need you for a while, but you can set up that contraption over there right outside the fence. What is it, anyhow?"

"It's called a service wagon. They're becoming very popular. Great for hauling ..."

"Yes, yes. Be ready with the water. There'd better be more than one bottle in there. These folks seem to inhale the contents of their water bottles."

"I'm on it," Marla told the woman's disappearing back.

The woman flounced off to confront a guy in his thirties with close-cropped blond hair who'd just arrived on court. He must've been another team member because he wore the requisite olive-green shirt and white shorts.

"Where have you been, Tanner? You were due here ten minutes ago," the woman said, her tone accusing.

Was she the team captain or whatever the leaders of pickleball teams were called? She certainly thought she was in charge.

"Sorry, Eloise. I had to stop by the post office to ship that package we didn't finish until late last night," Tanner said, trying to explain.

"Those sketches should've been ready to go by the close of day."

"You wouldn't release them until you personally checked each one, and you got called away until after seven."

"It should have been ready much earlier in the day, before I got called away."

He opened his mouth to reply, but Marla never heard whatever he'd been about to say because the woman he'd called Eloise had already pivoted to approach another player.

Marla pulled the wagon over to the spot Eloise had indicated. It didn't appear she had anything to do for a bit, but to be on the safe side, she checked the water supply to ensure none of the bottles had tipped over in transit.

Once she assured herself all was ready, she occupied herself observing the proceedings on the court. She settled into the folding chair Kitty had insisted she include and attempted to determine who was who.

"Marla! What brings you to our pickleball game? Don't tell me you've joined the team?"

The statuesque brunette who'd come up to her was one of the women she'd met at Kitty's book club. The one who was interested in Letitia's wardrobe. Marla attempted to recall the woman's name.

"Liz Parsons," the newcomer said, offering a slender, well-manicured hand. "We met at book club. I live in your condo building. On the first floor."

"Right. You're the one who wanted to know what wardrobe items I got to keep from the show."

"Guilty. I'm a bit of a fashionista."

Marla checked out Liz's playing clothes. "I can see. Even your uniform looks good on you."

Liz glanced down at what she was wearing. "This? Pure luck. My coloring is similar to that witch over there." She pointed to Eloise.

"Witch?" Marla had already figured that out for herself, but to hear a woman she hardly knew say it out loud was a bit of a shock.

Liz put a hand over her mouth. "Sorry. Is she a friend of yours?"

She laughed. "No. I just met her. Actually, we didn't really exchange names. She just caught me arriving with today's water, and I explained that I was subbing for Scottie."

"Oh, right. Scottie told me she wouldn't be here this week, but I didn't know she'd corralled you into replacing her. As for the witch, she goes by Eloise Wallace. I wouldn't worry about clashing with her. She'll be too busy harassing the team to pick on you unless you get in her way. She likes to think of herself as team captain, although we've never elected her. That would never happen. No one likes her, for a long list of reasons. But no one wants to be in charge, either. So we put up with her."

"Scottie didn't clue me in to any of that."

Now Liz laughed too. "Can you blame her? If you knew about Eloise, you most likely wouldn't have agreed to be here."

"You're probably right. Scottie wangled last-minute tickets to a Taylor Swift concert in Chicago, and I doubt she wanted to miss out," Marla replied. "I don't know anything about pickleball. Can you give me a headline version?"

"It'll have to be just that. Eloise is already eyeing me over here. We're part of the St. Paul Pickleball League. The game has become so popular, there are three pairs on each team. Each pair plays three games. The best two of the three win. This week we're playing a six-person team from Cottage Grove."

"Parsons! Get over here now," Eloise Wallace shouted from

across the court. "No time for chitchat. Your backhand needs more work after that poor performance last week."

"I rest my case. Sorry, gotta go," Liz said, taking off.

Years ago in high school, Marla had tried out for a girls' basketball team. She'd quickly discovered basketball wasn't her thing. Thanks to the ballet and tap lessons her parents had encouraged her to take, she moved her feet well. But her body, probably still adjusting to the sudden height increase, refused to recognize the connection between her hands and feet. She could dribble and shoot but not in sync with her feet. The coach had spent extra time with her, working on various hands-feet exercises. Finally, long after Marla had already realized basketball wasn't in her future, the coach sat her down privately and suggested, sweetly, that Marla find another sport.

Other sports didn't seem to be her bag either. Cross-country wore her out. Swimming triggered her allergies. That coach suggested she find another way to spend her after-school hours, so she tried out for a school play. To her relief, and her parents', everything seemed to come together when she walked onto her first stage. She not only remembered her lines, but stage directions came naturally. Her body had found its home.

She never would've made it through that gauntlet of athletic challenges if any of the coaches had come down on her case like this Eloise person was doing with her pickleball team. How would that affect their play?

It didn't take long to find out. And the results were not good. The guy, Tanner, was partnered with a woman who appeared to be fifteen or twenty years his senior. Although Marla had never seen the game played before, it was easy to tell the two weren't working well together by the way the woman kept moving in front of Tanner and from the exasperated looks he kept shooting her direction.

The first pair played two games. She had no idea what the

final score was, but from the way Eloise charged over to both of them afterwards, her face twisted in rage, it wasn't difficult to tell the outcome.

The pair toweled off and then slunk off the court.

"Hey, guys, good show out there," Marla told them when they popped over to meet her.

"What game were you watching?" a very dejected Tanner asked. "The two of us couldn't get it together."

"But thanks for the kind words, anyhow," the woman said. "I'm Nell Hampton. I shouldn't even be here today. The woman fired me two weeks ago, but I felt I owed it to the rest of the team to show up."

Talk about a double whammy. Losing the game was one thing, but to have also been so recently fired by the woman who'd put herself in charge of the team was quite another. Marla wasn't sure she could be so supportive of the team had it been her. "Believe it or not, I've been there myself recently," she replied.

Nell gave her a second look. "Omigod, you're that actress who played the PI. You got fired, too."

Marla offered her hand. "I'm Marla Dane. I played Letitia Carruthers on *Carruthers on the Case*. Technically, I wasn't fired. At least I don't call it that. I was replaced by another actress."

"A younger actress, as I recall."

Marla couldn't help but smile. No matter how little people seemed to know about her situation, they always seemed to recall the younger actress part. "Yes, that's me."

"What on earth are you doing here as Water Girl for our game?"

"I prefer Water Lady, if you don't mind," she replied, surprising herself with the subtlety.

"Good to know you're here," Tanner said, "although my container still has a little left."

Nell passed on a refill also. Then the two shuttled off to a nearby bench.

The next game began within a few minutes. This time, Eloise was paired with a guy about her age. "Let's not have a repeat of last week, Brecken," she told the man.

"Then don't cut off my shots," Brecken replied.

"I only did that because you were asleep at the wheel. Someone had to keep the volley going."

"I was no such thing. You just don't trust me."

The whistle blew, cutting off their comments. Was that their pregame windup, each egging the other on, or were they truly at odds with each other?

Sure enough, whatever had been going on between them didn't help their play. He seemed to hesitate before returning shots as if anticipating her taking over at the last second.

Like the last pair, these two were defeated as well. Eloise stormed off somewhere on her own, but the guy came over to Marla.

"You're new."

"I'm a sub," she replied.

"Thanks for helping out." He left it at that and wandered off to join the other two.

The next pair, Liz and another woman, actually worked together to score, redeeming the team in the third match. But when they won, Eloise was nowhere around to congratulate them.

"Thanks," the other woman, who appeared to be about the same age as Eloise, told Marla when she came over to her.

"You're welcome, but I don't know what for. No one has needed more water today."

"Your presence is reassuring, though. We appreciate your giving up several hours on a Saturday to help out. I'm Grace Adamson."

Marla immediately experienced a calming vibe as she gazed into Grace's friendly hazel eyes. "Nice to meet you. I'm Marla Dane."

"*The* Marla Dane?" Grace asked. "Well, of course you are. I can't believe I looked right at you and didn't realize it was you. In fact, I can't believe you're our water girl today."

"A favor to a friend, your regular."

"I'd heard you were in town, but I never dreamed you'd be at our game," Grace said.

"This court is on the grounds of the condo complex where I'm staying."

"Did you see where Eloise went right after the game?" Grace asked Liz as she joined them.

"Don't know and don't care, although my guess is she didn't know how to say, 'Great game, ladies,' and hustled off before she had to."

"It shouldn't surprise me that she wouldn't have a good word for me, but she could have congratulated you. We were the only ones to win one for the team today," Grace said.

"Dream on, Grace. Did she ever compliment you when you worked together?"

Grace pulled in her lips. "Not her style. I'd gotten used to her personality there, but you'd think she'd be a little more appreciative of everyone else's efforts on the court."

"You don't have to be on the team. The woman stole your company from you," Liz replied.

"You're right. But it's one way to keep in touch with you guys."

"It's your life. Only you know why you continue to put up with her."

With the third win, the day's matches seemed to be over, along with Marla's responsibility for the extra water, which went untouched. Even she hadn't been all that thirsty.

Everyone disappeared as fast as they'd shown up.

No need to pack up. Maybe she'd turn the untouched bottles over to Scottie for the next week.

She'd done her good deed. Time to head back to Kitty's condo and never again attend another pickleball game.

THANKS in large part to Marla's lesson in pie baking, Kitty survived her stint as a pie judge. In fact, at least according to her, the experience went quite well. The first forty-eight hours following the event, Marla was pleased for her sister. After that, not so much. And if she never heard the name Hub Sherman again, it would be too soon. Fortunately, Kitty didn't bring him back to her condo.

Marla didn't expect to see Scottie for a few days, figuring she stayed at least another day in Chicago. But she did think the woman would stop by or call on Monday to thank her for taking over her water role.

On Tuesday, instead of Scottie, she was visited by Colman Goodhue, the Maple Knolls Chief of Police. A tad taller than Marla, Goodhue also had reddish hair sprinkled with gray like her, only his gray was winning out sooner. His usually smiling gray eyes were more somber today.

"Chief, haven't seen you since we wrapped up the Elliot murder. Unless some new detail popped up?"

Goodhue had been all smiles after she and Rex discovered who killed the Condo Casanova, as the media tagged him. There were no smiles today.

"Could we sit somewhere?" he asked.

"Uh, sure." She led him to the sofa in the living room. She settled in a nearby easy chair.

"I understand you helped out at a pickleball match last Saturday."

"Yes, I subbed for the woman who usually provides the water for the team so she could go to Chicago."

"And you met a woman by the name of Eloise Wallace?" he continued.

"Yes, but just briefly. She acts as the team's captain and went off right away to get things organized."

"Had you met her before?"

"No." His seriousness alarmed her. "What's this all about, Chief?"

"She was murdered, Marla."

four

. . .

"Murdered?" Marla asked, not tracking.

"Poisoned," Chief Goodhue replied.

"Poisoned? Are you sure?"

"Not a hundred percent. We're waiting for the autopsy and toxicology report to come back, but it looks like that. Most likely from arsenic. Skin jaundiced as well as the sclera of the eyes; signs of foam at the mouth, although mostly dried up, meaning she'd been dead for some time. I'll spare you the rest of the unpleasant details, but there were no other signs of physical attack.

"Her assistant, a guy named Tanner Oliver, found her midday yesterday. She didn't come in to work. She ran Essy, a public relations firm in St. Paul. The official name is Springboard Concepts, a mouthful. So that's been abbreviated to SC and spelled out as Essy. According to Oliver, it was a rare day when she didn't beat everyone else to work. He got worried when she didn't show up by eleven. She had a client meeting scheduled for noon."

"I'm sorry to hear of her death, but what does it have to do with me?" she asked.

He straightened in his seat before replying. "You may have been one of the last people to see her alive. I heard you were in charge of handing out water to the players."

She jerked forward. "Omigod! You don't think I had something to do with poisoning her?"

He shook his head. "No. At least not until we know more. But no one on her team seems to have seen her since the last game was over. She apparently just disappeared."

Marla made herself stop and go through Saturday's events in her head. "I only spoke with her when I arrived. That was maybe all of a minute. Unlike the rest of the team, she didn't approach me the rest of the time for water or any other reasons. She was too busy directing traffic on the court."

He eyed her. "Were you expressing your opinion of her in that last comment?"

"Sorry. I shouldn't have said that. I only met her that morning."

"But you didn't like her?"

"Not really, but not enough to poison her! Just enough to stay out of her way as much as I could."

He sat back, relaxed his shoulders. "I thought that was about what you'd say, but I wanted you to confirm it for me."

"Does that mean I'm not a suspect?"

"You're not completely off the hook until we confirm what the poison was and how it was administered, although we suspect it could have been in one of her water bottles. We still haven't even established the time of death. From what little I know about poisons, some are fast-acting, and some take a while to act. If it was poison, though, we know it was enough of a dose to take her out pretty fast."

"Have you called in the state people?" she asked. He'd chosen to use the state and the St. Paul authorities to a certain degree with the Elliot murder but mainly for technical support. He'd turned to her and Rex to do the investigating.

"Remains to be seen," he replied. He paused, not eyeing her.

Surely he wouldn't ask Rex and her for help again? Especially so soon after the Elliot case. Yes, they'd identified that killer. And in just a few days. But they'd also come face to face with death when they confronted the killer, a situation she wanted to avoid in the future at all costs. She'd never been so scared.

"The state people are already working on the poison angle. But I'm still short-staffed, and the few officers I have are either preparing the initial case reports or wrapping up the details from the Elliot case. If we can completely clear you as a suspect, I'd like your help again since you observed her interactions that last day she was known to be alive."

"Are you serious? Rex and I got lucky with the Elliot case. I have absolutely no investigative training nor has Rex ever been a homicide investigator. Surely the St. Paul or Minneapolis police can deal with this murder?"

His gaze went everywhere in the room except to look at her directly. Before replying, he let out a drawn-out breath. "Yes, they could. But I would prefer this case not get the higher profile it would receive if it were handled by the larger departments."

"But they have the resources. And their people are experienced," she replied, not following his line of thought.

"True. But put yourself in my shoes. Our small town that's never had a homicide has now been confronted with two within weeks of each other. Horrible for the victims, of course, but also an embarrassment for Maple Knolls. What does this say about the safety of our little community to outsiders, to potential home buyers?"

What did it say about him as chief of police? That's what he was really thinking, although he hadn't put it in words.

But wouldn't he protect his reputation more if he handed it off to a group that had the resources? And if they couldn't solve the murder or if it took forever to solve it, wouldn't he be able to hide behind them? Keeping the case on his home turf might give him more control, but he'd be leaving himself wide open to criticism if she and Rex couldn't produce. Not to mention the pressure she and Rex would be facing.

Rex. "Have you spoken to Rex yet?" she asked, hoping her one-time partner would turn him down in no uncertain terms.

"Rex? Yes, I have."

"And?" She didn't care for his evasiveness.

"Rex is on board, provided we meet two conditions. We have to clear you from suspicion. That accomplished, which I have no doubt we'll do, then you have to agree to join him as his partner. And I'll add a third. We'll reimburse you for your time. Not the big bucks you're used to in the entertainment world, but it's a step toward acknowledging the professional job you'll be expected to do."

So much for Rex getting them out of this.

"Besides me, do you have any suspects yet?" she asked.

"From the initial case reports my officers have put together, it would appear anyone on that pickleball team might have killed her. Five people. That's a lot for you to concentrate on, but that's another reason why I want you involved. You witnessed them in action."

"You think one of the people on the team killed her?"

He shrugged. "Maybe. It's a place to start. If none of them seems likely after we've questioned them, perhaps one or more of them can suggest a likely suspect."

"How do we clear me? I know I didn't poison her. I didn't even serve her. But how do I prove that?"

"We ask Rex for help again."

"Rex? He wasn't there. I don't know if he knew her or not."

"Let's assume he didn't. And since he wasn't there, he can be objective about your part in this."

Interesting thought. Was she ready to work with Rex again so soon? More to the point, could she work with Rex if he was investigating her?

"I thought the only reason Rex agreed to investigate the Elliot murder with me was that he owed you for something that happened in the past. Why is he willing to sign on again this time?"

"I can't believe you have to ask," the chief replied. "You and Rex may have started out as adversaries, but by the time the two of you faced the killer's gun, you'd become a team. You each respected the other. All Rex had to hear is that you might, *might*, mind you, be a suspect in this case, and he was ready to volunteer his services to prove your innocence."

That caught her attention. She and Rex had signed off on the Elliot case on good terms, but she hadn't seem much of him since then. But according to Goodhue, Rex would consider pairing up again.

"Do I have your permission to tell him to proceed?" Goodhue asked.

"What does he think about my being a suspect?" Learning the answer to that question suddenly became very important.

"Told me I was a fool to think you could ever poison anyone."

Rex really said that? "Wait, then how can he objectively investigate me if he already thinks I'm innocent?"

"That opinion is just for you and me to know. Rex's training as a police officer will kick in. He'll be fair. So fair, you'll probably wind up hating him before he concludes what your role was in all this. Be prepared. He won't appear sympathetic because he can't be. Don't hold it against him or fight him because of it."

Former police officer Rex Alcorn was about to investigate her. The idea was so far from the way this day had begun. What if Rex wasn't convinced of her innocence? That was crazy. She was innocent. That was the bedrock of whatever happened from here on. Goodhue didn't have any choice but to consider her as a suspect, whether Rex was involved or not.

"Okay. Give him the go-ahead. Do I need to go to your office so it's official?"

He studied her. "That won't be necessary."

"I'm not crazy to have found myself in this position, but having Rex investigate me seems to be the best alternative."

REX WAS at her door within an hour of her giving Goodhue the go-ahead. Though it had only been days since they were last together, seeing him again so soon now was a surprising pleasure. Tiny drops of moisture from a recent shower dotted his short, graying brown hair, and he smelled yummy, like sandalwood, whether it was cologne, aftershave or soap. His gray-blue eyes were even bluer than she remembered thanks to the blue chambray shirt he wore.

"Thought you came to Minnesota to get away from the dramatics," he said, settling onto the sofa before being told to make himself at home.

"And how are you, too?" she replied. "I had no idea pickleball could draw me into another murder."

"Your way of telling me you're innocent?"

"If you want to take it as such. Or you can ask me outright if I killed the woman. The answer would be the same. A resounding no."

"I'll get around to that in a bit. First, let's start with how you wound up handing out water at the game. You never said you were into pickleball."

"I wasn't, and from here on, I'm definitely not." She related how Scottie Richards had begged her to sub for her so she could go see her idol.

"Where was Kitty in all this? Pickleball sounds more like her," he asked.

"Haven't you heard? Kitty is now a pie-baking judge." She filled him in on Kitty's latest love interest.

He chuckled. "I continue to be amazed at the lengths she'll go to when it comes to her social life."

She started to tell him how she'd tried and failed to demonstrate making a pie for Kitty as prep for her new task but cut herself off before she revealed her problems with videocasting. "I never should've let Scottie talk me into taking her place until I made her tell me everything that was involved. At the time, it seemed like a no-brainer until I got to wondering about it later."

"Wondering about what?" he asked. So far, he was letting her take her own time reliving the experience.

"Providing water sounded easy enough, especially since everyone brought their own water container to start with, but was there a special brand I should purchase? How many games did they play? Had I committed myself to a full day of work?"

"Give me a little more detail about the water," he said.

"What more is there to know about bottled water? Spring water. I was told to bring two large bottles. I took three for good measure, forty-eight ounces each."

"How did you serve it?"

"I didn't. Apparently whatever they'd brought in their own bottles was enough for them."

"You didn't open any of your bottles?"

"No."

His interest in the water continued. "Was that typical? No

one needed additional water even though you were there with plenty more?"

"I couldn't say whether that was typical, since it was my first time, although Scottie said something about my being there was only for backup."

"Where did they drink their water?" he asked.

She tried to recall. "It appeared that except when they were actually playing, everyone on the team had their own bottle in hand. I'm not sure, but I think their bottles were set off to the side of the court along with their equipment bags when they were playing."

He considered her words a few beats before his next question. "I've never played the game or seen it played, but it would seem you'd need quite a big water bottle to get through the day."

"You're right. They were huge. I'm guessing thirty ounces at least."

"All you provided, or were prepared to provide, was water, right? No snacks?"

"I just brought the water. They each brought their own snacks, I assume because they each preferred different foods. I saw someone with a slice of watermelon. Someone else had a granola bar."

He reached in his pants pocket and pulled out a paper. "These are the players on the team." He read off the names. "Did I mention anyone you didn't talk to?"

"No. There were six players on the team. At least that's all who showed up Saturday. They may have substitutes."

"And to be clear, you didn't serve Eloise Wallace?"

"No, I did not."

He rose and paced around the room. She recognized this mannerism from their prior investigation. Something was on his mind, but it either hadn't fully shaped or he was deciding how to tell her.

"Rex? What are you thinking?"

He returned to his seat and faced her. "Until we know for sure which poison killed her, we can't make any definitive assumptions. If she was poisoned at the game, it didn't take effect immediately. But the fact that no one seems to know what happened to her or where she went right after the third match suggests it could've have started to kick in then."

"Any idea when the results will come in?"

He shook his head. "Hopefully yet today."

"Then I'm still under suspicion?" She knew the answer but wanted him to confirm it.

"Yeah. Once I receive confirmation that none of them got any water or anything else from you, you should be off the hook. While we wait, I'd like to talk to Kitty and Scottie Richards."

"Them? Why? They weren't there."

"I've gotta do this by the book, Marla. Check out your story."

"Not the team?"

He put the list of team names away. "Not yet. When do you expect Kitty home?"

"It's hard to say these days, when she's off with Hub Sherman. Want me to call her?"

"I will," he replied.

Kitty answered immediately. The call lasted all of two minutes. "She's on her way home and agreed to meet me in ten minutes at my condo," he told Marla once he hung up.

"In other words, you don't want me to overhear what you ask her."

"Like I said, by the book. You have to remain here on the sidelines for now."

"What if ...?"

He held up a hand. "Just be patient. Okay? This shouldn't take long."

Rex would be fair. She had no doubt about that. For now, that was all she could ask.

five

. . .

Kitty showed up thirty minutes later, shaking her head but wearing a grin. "How do you do it, Marla?" she asked as she retrieved an ice cream bar from the fridge.

"Do what?" Marla asked, taking the bait.

"All you had to do was buy some big bottles of water, take them to the pickleball match and serve it to whoever needed it. The next thing I know, you're a suspect in a murder case. Not a fictional PI or even a real consulting investigator for the police. A suspect, like in they think you might've killed a woman. You can no longer accuse me of being the one whose life is topsy-turvy."

"I take it you've met with Rex and he filled you in on all the gory details?"

"I doubt I know the whole story. Rex doesn't part with information that easily. But I got enough of the picture to know the police think you might've offed the poor woman. How did you even meet her? You've hardly been here long enough to develop a list of enemies."

"I only met her Saturday before the match. And I wouldn't

even count that as meeting her. She approached me as soon as I arrived at the pickleball court demanding to know who I was and took off before I could introduce myself. She didn't even remember Scottie's name. Once she knew the water part was covered, she was off."

Kitty licked her ice cream treat. "Rex wanted to know how you'd found yourself giving out water. I could only recount what you'd told me the day Scottie asked you to sub for her. Beyond that, all I could tell him was about our trip to the grocery store to purchase the bottles of water. And of course the ingredients for a couple apple pies. Apparently you told him about my being a pie-baking judge and that you'd demonstrated how to bake a pie to me, since I was never very good at that. The idea of you as a pie maker surprised him. Even tickled him a bit. He wanted to know if there was any left for him."

"Tell me you didn't mention my miserable attempt at a video."

"Not exactly." She didn't go on.

"How *not exactly*?" Marla asked.

"I sort of told him we'd used your pie-baking demo as a means of producing your own video."

"Kitty! You knew I didn't want Rex to know about my failure."

"It was Rex, Marla. You know how he can get you to reveal things. The part about the video was out of my mouth before I could stop it. But wait, I didn't say a thing about how it went."

"What about Tom Casey? Did you happen to mention him?"

"Well, I had to, once the subject of videocasting arose. I didn't want Rex to think we'd put one together on our own."

"No, you wouldn't want to do that, would you?" Marla couldn't keep the sarcasm out of her tone.

"Don't sound so touchy. Why do you care if Rex knows you tried your hand at making your own video? All you have to tell him, if he even asks, is that it didn't seem to be your cup of tea." She seemed so satisfied with her reply, it wasn't worth getting upset with her. Besides, the videocasting thing wasn't the main point. "What did you tell him about me being a possible poisoner?"

Kitty ran her tongue along the wooden stick, drawing in all the remaining chocolate. "What do you think I said? That you'd never resort to killing another person, no matter what way, and that he and the police were wasting valuable time considering you a suspect when they should be looking for the real killer."

Leave it to Kitty to come to her defense. She had no doubt her sister had done a great job of being justly outraged that Marla was the least bit under suspicion.

"Thanks. That's the important part. Did he appear to believe you?"

"This was Rex I was talking to. I had no way to read his mind, but on the other hand, he was duly impressed with your help identifying Drake Elliot's killer. He respects your judgment. If you didn't serve water to anyone Saturday, he'll believe it." She blinked as an idea hit. "Did you show him that you still had all three bottles we bought?"

Marla cringed. "Don't you remember? I refrigerated one, and we each had a glass on Sunday."

Kitty's shoulder slumped. "Sorry. Forgot." A new idea hit. "But we survived. That proves there was nothing in there."

Marla played with the idea. "How could I possibly poison an unopened bottle? Hold on. That could prove my innocence. You saw all three unopened bottles after I brought them home. I can't remember—were you in the room when I opened the one?"

Kitty rubbed a cheek, trying to remember. "That's right! I was out here in the kitchen when you offered me a glass. It didn't hit me at the time, but you pulled it from a brand-new bottle in the fridge and opened it."

Marla closed her eyes in relief. Finally, a witness. "Did you tell Rex about seeing me open the bottle?"

"Uh, no. I thought it best to answer his questions as briefly as possible. I didn't add anything. Not my usual behavior, I know, but this was you we were discussing. And whether you poisoned another person."

True, it wasn't Kitty's typical behavior, but her sister could be quite logical and reasonable when the situation called for it. "Thanks. But if that question was never asked, Rex still needs to know."

Kitty grabbed her phone. "I'll get right on that."

Marla held up her hand. "Better me than you. If you call him, it will look like we've been discussing what you told him."

"Which we have," Kitty replied, perplexed.

"True, but I don't want it to look like you changed your testimony to help me. I'll ask him if he asked you the next time I see him."

That seemed to appease Kitty. "Now that that's settled, I need to get ready for my date tonight."

"It's ten in the morning. You already look great."

"Some of the Prairie Harvest Flour bigwigs are in town. Hub's taking me to a private dinner party."

"Wow. Things between the two of you seem to be moving fast."

"You think so? I like him, true. Our senses of humor are in sync. And he knows so much about so many things and so many people. And either he is well off or he has a healthy expense account. I like going to plays and concerts and eating at great restaurants. Plus, he's not bad to look at. But I'm not in the market for either a new husband or even a serious relationship. I'm still in recovery mode from Gardner Lovejoy's peccadilloes." Even though Kitty had been divorced for a number of years, her former husband's taking up with another woman still rankled.

"Just let me know if things change and you want this Hub guy to move in and me to move out," Marla said. She rather liked living here with Kitty, but she preferred not to trip over a live-in boyfriend. Kitty might trust him, but she didn't need to court potential leaks to the media.

Rex showed up around noon, bringing with him deli sandwiches for the two of them. Kitty was already ensconced in her room getting ready for the evening's activity. "I've now talked to both your sister and Scottie Richards. Scottie sends her apologies for not getting back to you as soon as she returned from Chicago. She told me she was exhausted from a weekend of catching up with relatives and partying."

"She just texted me with that same apology. Tell me you didn't chide her for being so slow with her thanks."

"Okay, I won't. I merely hinted that a text was the least she could do, but not until after I'd learned what she knew about your role in this murder case."

"Did she already know about Eloise Wallace's death?"

"Hard to keep that out of the news, even though Goodhue's been attempting exactly that."

"Did she confirm my story about why I was there?" Marla asked, when he hadn't already brought it up.

"Yeah. I still can't believe she had the gall to ask you. She barely knows you. Apparently, and don't be offended, she'd asked several other people to step in for her before she got to you."

"That really cheers me up," she joked.

"Actually, it helped your case. Showed you hadn't inserted yourself there on purpose. As you told me before, you were simply helping out a friend—rather, an acquaintance."

"Now that you've talked to both my sister and Scottie, am I cleared of suspicion?"

He folded his hands and then ran one of them down a pants leg. He was wearing khaki slacks today. Stalling? Not yet ready to give her good news? Or just drawing out the suspense? The latter didn't sound like Rex, but as it turned out, he was simply picking his words.

"Both women swore you'd never attended a pickleball game before, let alone met Eloise Wallace. Both also confirmed that your only role there was the dispensing of water for the players if they needed additional hydration beyond whatever their individual water bottles contained. Despite the fact neither actually saw you there, it would appear you had nothing to do with the murder. I could be a hundred percent sure with direct witness testimony, which is the crux of my problem."

"Just ask the team if anyone got water from me," she said.

"Which I intend to do. But Goodhue also wants you to participate in those interrogations." He stared at her. "You see my dilemma? You can't be part of those questions until we know for sure you're clear."

"But I am clear! Kitty was with me when I bought three large bottles of water and helped me put them in the service wagon she loaned me. She also saw that I brought all three unopened containers home."

He cocked his head. "She didn't mention that part."

"Did you ask her directly if she saw me arrive home with three unopened bottles?"

"Un, no." He scratched his head. "How did I miss that? I'm thorough in my questioning."

Marla tried to picture the scene, Rex interrogating Kitty. "Did she receive any calls or texts during your meeting?"

He scrunched up his brow. "Come to think of it, yeah. That

guy you said she'd been seeing. She got all excited about some event he invited her to and asked if we were done."

Marla nodded. She might only have been in town a short time, but her familiarity with her sister's habits had already returned.

"I'm sorry, Marla. That shouldn't have happened. I'm better than that. It's just that Kitty ..."

"Is Kitty? I understand. But does that information help my case?"

"It goes a long way," he replied. "Show me the three unopened bottles, and you're exonerated."

She was afraid he'd say something like that. "I can't. We opened one the other day and drank some of the contents. It was just there sitting in the fridge, and we both were thirsty," she rushed to say.

"Why are you making this so difficult for me?"

"More for myself than you," she said. "But she can swear to seeing me return with three unopened bottles and to hearing me open the one. Surely that's conclusive enough evidence?"

Rex rolled his eyes. "I need to interview Kitty again. Where is she?"

"Getting ready for her hot date tonight. You know, that event she got so excited about earlier?"

"Can you get her to come out here?"

"Now?"

He narrowed his eyes. "The sooner I talk to her, the sooner we can move ahead with this investigation."

Marla found Kitty just toweling off from her shower. It took some convincing to get her sister to appear in a terrycloth robe without makeup, but Kitty finally agreed to talk to Rex after several less than subtle reminders from Marla that she might be headed to jail if Kitty didn't substantiate her story.

Once Kitty arrived in the kitchen to chat with Rex, Marla excused herself and went to her room.

He knocked on her door ten minutes later, and she invited him in. "Would you believe she actually accused me of doing a shoddy job of clearing your name?"

"She doesn't like her beauty prep to be disturbed by anything, even when it comes to proving my innocence. But she did verify the condition of the bottles, didn't she?"

"Yes. I wish you hadn't opened that one, but she swears she saw you do it and that it had been full and unopened at the time." He checked his watch. "It's just early afternoon. We still have time to track down most if not all of the team."

"Now? Just like that?" she asked, not having anticipated starting so soon.

"I have to make a call to Goodhue to get his blessing, then we're off."

six

. . .

Someone knocked on the front door while Rex was in the kitchen calling Goodhue. Marla answered it to find Liz there. By the pinched set to her eyes, the visitor wasn't there on a friendly house call. "Good! I was hoping to find you home," Liz said, settling onto the sofa Marla indicated.

Was her showing up good news or bad news? She'd been the first team player Marla had seen on Saturday. "You're here to see me and not Kitty?" she asked her visitor.

"That's right. I want to hire you to investigate Eloise Wallace's death."

"I think you're confusing me with the character I played on TV. I'm an actress."

"You found out who killed Drake Elliot. I'm asking you to do the same for me."

Marla sank into a nearby easy chair. "That was a fluke, Liz. Since the guy lived here in the building, the chief of police thought I'd have better access to those who might be suspected in his death. That, plus I could trade on my celebrity to encourage folks to talk to me."

"I also live in this building, and I was there Saturday. As far as I'm concerned, you're still a celebrity."

"You give me too much credit. Rex Alcorn played a large role in tracking down the killer," Marla replied.

"But you helped him."

How would she react to the news she was about to deliver? "I can't accept your offer because I've already been contacted by Police Chief Goodhue and asked to consult on this case also."

"Are the two of you partnering up again?"

"Yes, although that's just been decided, so it would be premature to tell anyone at this point."

"Then I guess you'll be talking to me soon, only not as your client." Liz's voice was barely above a whisper.

"We'll wait, if you need time to find someone else to represent you."

"Like an attorney? At least not at this time. I didn't kill her." She stopped abruptly. "Omigod! I called her a 'witch' when I first saw you that day."

"Maybe it's best you say nothing more until Rex and I talk to you in our semiofficial capacity."

Liz hastily got to her feet. "You're right. I hate the idea of appearing to be on two different sides, though."

"If what you said about not killing her is true, and at this point I have no reason to doubt you, then we're on the same side, that of finding the truth."

"When should I expect you?" Liz asked.

"Probably sometime today, once Rex and I get our act together."

Liz made her way to the door. "Later, then."

Later, right. What had she agreed to?

"LIZ WANTED to hire you to discover who killed Eloise Wallace and clear her name?" Rex asked a few minutes later after Marla brought him up to date.

"Are you hurt that she didn't come to you?" she asked, half joking.

"I'm doing my best to hide my tears."

"Not so long ago you were praising me for solving the Elliot case. With your assistance, of course."

"Assistance?" His voice rose.

"Okay, with your experience and great intellect. Satisfied?"

"Better. But back to my question. Did you pick up on any particular vibes behind her asking?"

She tilted her head to consider what he'd asked. "I get the idea she came to me not because of my—our success with our prior case but for some other reason. Although that is how she couched her offer. You're suggesting she had an ulterior motive?"

"Not suggesting. Asking you," he replied.

"Do you think she anticipated my being asked to team up with you again by Chief Goodhue and this was a strategic move to cut me off at the pass?"

"Just asking. What do you think?"

"Interesting theory. Fortunately, she was too late. But I might've given her offer more serious consideration if you, the chief and I hadn't already talked. Do you think she's worried she'll be charged with the murder?"

"We won't know until we've talked to her officially. Maybe not, probably not even then. But she's given us a place to start."

Liz was waiting for them when they knocked on her door ten minutes later. "I'm sure Marla told you about my earlier visit," she said before they brought it up. Another attempt to cut them off at the pass?

"She mentioned it, yes," Rex replied. "That was very clever."

"Clever?" she returned. "I'm rarely accused of that trait. Where did that come from?"

"Rex and I both wonder if you anticipated my being part of the investigation and you wanted to make it impossible for me to participate by tying me up before I got the offer," Marla said.

Liz started to say something and then stopped. "Oh. Yes, I can see how that might make me appear to be very clever. The thing is ... I thought if you were looking into the case on my behalf, we could get to know each other better."

Had she gone into fangirl mode? Such behavior was not unfamiliar to Marla, although she hadn't experienced it in months. "You didn't need the ruse of hiring me to get to know me better, Liz. I've hardly seen you since the book club lunch. Why haven't you stopped by just to say hi?"

Liz glanced at her shoes. "I, uh you're a big star and I'm not. But when I saw you handling the water last Saturday, I realized you were approachable. But then all this ugliness with Eloise's murder happened. All I could think to do was ask you to clear my name instead of coming to you to talk about my fashion ideas."

"Fashion ideas?" Marla asked. She exchanged a quick glance at Rex. Neither had expected that kind of response.

Liz stuck out her chin before replying. "That's right. I design and fabricate clothes on the side." Her tone was between prideful and defensive. "Women's fashions. Primarily cocktail dresses and evening wear. Most retailers haven't gotten the message that prom dresses of the seventies are out, except for those selling prom dresses, who think their clients are showgirls. Or have no idea what to make for girls with less than perfect figures."

Unable to think of an immediate comeback, Marla let her go on.

Liz seemed to realize she'd been rambling and stopped

short. "Sorry. Guess I've been practicing my spiel so much in my head, the first part just rolled out. Anyway, yes, I had an ulterior motive for coming to you, Marla, but that was it. Not to prevent you from consulting for the police."

Rex shifted his weight. "Now that you've shared why you approached Marla, let's move on to the reason we're here."

"Which is ... to grill me?" Liz said.

"This will be a lot easier for all three of us if you drop that attitude, Liz," Rex told her, his official voice now quite evident. "We want to know what you observed at the games last Saturday."

"As well as any insights you might have about the victim and anyone else that was there," Marla added.

"Yeah, I know. Where do you want me to start?"

"Tell us everything you can remember about Saturday, starting with your arrival," Rex said.

"Let's all sit first," Liz replied. "This may take a while."

Marla and Rex settled on one end of Liz's turquoise L-shaped sectional. Liz went to the other end.

"I arrived a half hour earlier than my usual time because I wanted to get in extra practice time. Eloise had been harping about my backhand needing more work. We don't really get much of a warm-up period on game days because the other team is already there. Our team usually practices late Wednesday afternoons, but Eloise hadn't been satisfied with my progress and strongly suggested I return on my own on Thursday or Friday. But my day job—I'm an investment consultant—demanded my attention. The stock market has been fluctuating more than usual lately, and I needed to analyze the health of my clients' portfolios."

Liz had already revealed more than just the time of her arrival on Saturday. "We'll talk more about your chronology in a minute, but first, tell us why Eloise was concerned about your backhand. Was she the team's captain or trainer?" Marla asked.

"No, definitely not!" Liz replied with unexpected vehemence. "The team never voted on it. In fact, the role of captain was never discussed. Eloise just assumed she was in charge, and no one ever challenged her about it. Not directly, anyhow. You met her that day. I saw her talking to you. She wasn't the kind of person you said no to unless you were prepared to do battle with her."

"I never met Ms. Wallace. Why don't you explain for me why no one felt they could say no to the woman," Rex said.

"Take my situation, for instance. I knew Eloise way back and hadn't run into her in years until a few months ago. She could be quite ingratiating when she wanted to be. She was all smiles and compliments about my hair and clothes. My ego needed a boost that day after I'd nearly lost a client because we couldn't agree on a stock she wanted to purchase. When Eloise invited me to join her pickleball team, I was ripe for the picking.

"She only invited me because I could get her access to the pickleball courts here at Rambling Meadows. I guess in the first few minutes we were getting reacquainted I must have mentioned living here. Looking back, I can't believe I said yes. I played a little tennis years ago, but I was never that good at it. I was out of shape. I didn't realize I'd be committing my Wednesday afternoons and a good part of my Saturdays for the next several months, especially when I quickly learned this sport wasn't as easy as others claimed.

"I guess I assumed she was the one in charge, since she'd invited me to join the team without consulting anyone else. It wasn't until I'd been playing with them a couple times that I learned she considered herself the self-appointed leader. That was from one of the other team members, Grace Adamson, her former partner. I didn't know about that relationship until one of the other team members, I forget who, clued me in. I recall wondering out loud why Grace had remained on the team—now I remember. It was Nell, who still worked for Eloise—and she said something about no one being able to leave the team unless she kicked them off.

"I thought her comment odd, but I didn't press. That was before Eloise started attacking my game. Last month, I'd reached what I thought was the end of my tolerance of the heavy-handed way she treated everyone else on the team and told her I was quitting. I'd give her two weeks to find a replacement for me. She did a one-eighty in the way she treated me. That day. In the course of her begging me to stay, she revealed she needed me because of my affiliation with this condo complex. She must have realized immediately what a misstep that was because she then asked how her public relations firm could help my career. I made the mistake of mentioning my fashion design dream, and she took full advantage of it, promising to help me launch my line."

"And have you?" Marla asked, getting caught up in Liz's plans and almost forgetting the investigation.

Liz's lips curved into a hopeful smile. "Almost. But any help Eloise might have given me is a thing of the past."

Which was probably why Liz had suddenly gained enough chutzpah to approach her.

Marla couldn't help comparing Eloise Wallace's hold over Liz to some of the unhealthier symbiotic relationships she knew about in LA. People used other people. That seemed to be a fact of life in the network-driven culture in which she'd had to survive as an actor.

"Okay, you've given us some background about your relationship with the victim," Rex said, cutting off further discussion about Liz's future as a fashion designer. "Let's get back to this past Saturday. You told us you got there early. Were you able to get in your backhand practice?"

"Not at first. Eloise and Tanner and Nell were already there. Arguing. In the kitchen, that's the front area of the court. Actually, it was Eloise and Nell who were at it. Tanner, in his usual hanger-on manner, just stood there a foot away from them, taking it all in."

"Arguing? Like how? About what?" Marla asked.

"Can't help you there, I'm afraid. As soon as she saw me, Eloise stuck out her hand and told me to keep away. When I pointed out that they didn't appear to be doing anything related to pickleball, she actually snorted and turned back to their quarrel like I didn't even exist."

"How long did they remain there?" Rex asked.

"For most of my practice time. They got quieter for a bit, most likely due to my presence, and then they seemed to forget about me and got louder with a lot more gesturing. I got a telephone call from my mom about then—she never can remember I'm tied up for several hours on Saturdays—and I walked away from the court to talk to her. When I returned a few minutes later, Nell was no longer on the court. Tanner had moved closer and appeared to be trying to calm her. Grace and Brecken, Eloise's ex, had arrived by then and were engrossed in a much quieter discussion with Nell outside the court."

"Was that typical?" Marla asked.

"You mean all the fireworks and secret councils?" Liz replied. "Sort of, but last Saturday was a little more intense than usual."

"Any idea why?" Marla asked.

Liz ran her hands back through her hair. "I'm guessing it had something to do with Eloise's company, and since Nell was so incensed, it might have concerned Eloise's firing her two weeks ago. The woman's still getting over the recent death of her wife."

This was getting complicated. This "team" seemed to be a

team in name only. They certainly hadn't been pulling together on the pickleball court. "Where does Brecken, the husband, fit in all this?" Marla asked.

"Ex-husband," Liz replied. "I don't know for sure, but my bet would be he's backing Nell and Grace. His divorce from Eloise wasn't amicable."

Rex beat Marla to the punch on the next question. "That being the case, why was he on the team?"

Liz raised her hands surrender-style. "Beats me. Why did any of us stay on the team? I, uh, told you my reason. You barely met Eloise. She was a very compelling woman. There seemed to be a force field surrounding her that dared anyone who defied her to back down."

Marla had to agree, although she'd save that opinion to share with Rex later and not tell Liz now. For as brief a time as she'd been in contact with Eloise Wallace, the woman definitely matched Liz's description.

seven

. . .

lthough Marla and Rex continued to question Liz a few more minutes, they learned nothing new.

"Your thoughts?" Rex asked after they'd returned to his condo to regroup.

"I still haven't figured out if that question just after we finish interviewing someone is because you're really interested in what I think or if you're debating what you should think."

He turned a sardonic smile on her. "I'm disappointed. Thought you'd be onto that trick before now. Humor me. What are you thinking?"

"Two things. First, about Liz herself. I think everything she told us was the truth, at least in her mind. But I don't think she told us everything. There was more to her relationship with Eloise than she let on, otherwise I can't believe she would've stayed with the team just on some nebulous hope that the woman would help her develop her fashion business."

"I'm with you there. We keep digging into her background. What about the second thing?"

"According to Liz's description of her teammates, there's a big undercurrent of discontent amongst them. The same might be said of any group of six people, except four of them have worked together until recently and the fifth was the victim's husband. We need to strategize how and when to approach each of them, or they could likely circle the wagons to keep us from learning anything definitive about them."

"Do you think they might all be in this together?" he asked in response to her insights.

"I wasn't saying that, although it's possible. But I can't help thinking each of them had his or her own reason for remaining on the team. Those reasons could lead us to the real killer. We just have to pick away at them until we find the right one."

"Pick. Good word for our challenge. These interconnections on the team are like a human version of the game of pickup sticks."

That was a new one from him. "Pickup sticks?"

"Haven't you ever played that game?" he responded.

"When I was a kid. But I do remember how. You're suggesting we find the weakest link?"

"That's another game. We're not looking for strength here but the least connectedness. From Liz's description of the team, that sounds like the ex to me."

She envisioned the prone bodies of all five team members, Liz included, laid out across each other like sticks. For the moment, Liz's body was positioned off to the side. Brecken Wallace was a little closer to the cluster of the other three although set slightly apart. "Thanks for putting that image in my brain. Now I can't get it out."

"Let's see how it works. You may not have to."

Twenty minutes later, they caught up with Brecken Wallace, the ex-husband, at his home, an apartment in the old part of St. Paul. "I thought when we signed the divorce papers six years ago I would no longer have anything to do with that woman," he told them.

Though he'd been playing pickleball weekly for some time and apparently worked outdoors in his landscaping business, Brecken was at least fifteen pounds overweight. Not fat, but rounded with no sharp angles. His nondescript sandy brown hair suggested he hadn't seen a barber or a stylist in some time.

"But since she had no next of kin, the job of arranging her funeral and all came to me. What a joke on both of us, huh? She hasn't wanted anything to do with me since we split."

"How long were you married?" Marla asked.

"Seven years. I was working in facilities management at a local manufacturing plant at the time, which is where we met. She was an accounting tech in the main office. We were both laid off when the company downsized nine years ago. One of my coworkers, who'd also been laid off, and I started our own landscaping business, mainly mowing residential lawns in summer and snow removal in winter. I'm actually the one who suggested Eloise to Grace, who owned Essy. I knew Grace in high school.

"Bad move on my part, although at the time it seemed like the answer to our prayers. I was pleased for her those first few years as she dug in and learned the business. During that time, we'd been trying to start our family, but nature wasn't on our side. She gave up after two miscarriages. That's when she turned all that hurt and disappointment toward advancing at Essy. Long before Grace sold it to her, Eloise was thinking of it as her company.

"She changed during that time and became a person I didn't know. Not just ambitious but demanding and difficult to live with. It took another year for me to realize the marriage was dead."

"But you played on the same pickleball team with her," Rex pointed out now that Brecken had given them an overview of their marriage.

"One of the highlights of my life," Brecken replied sardonically.

"Explain," Marla said.

"I'm not a kept man, though it may look that way. Eighteen months ago, I needed some extra cash to expand my landscaping business. Until then, it had been a two-man operation focusing on small residences in the city. But a friend, who's the facilities manager at a small plumbing parts business in Apple Valley, asked if I'd like to help maintain their exterior, and I got excited at the possibility of growing the business. Excited enough that I was willing to humble myself with Eloise and ask for a loan. Just my luck, after putting up with her all those years, she had the nerve to win the lottery after we were divorced, so I had no claim to that money."

"And she turned you down?" Marla asked.

"I knew going in that she wouldn't make it easy for me. She'd wanted the divorce as much as I had, but it still bugged her ego that any man could walk away from her. Out of desperation, I kept approaching her, and about six months ago I got my money. But I had to join the team first. I can't explain why she was so into the game. She'd never been much for sports in the past, but having her own team seemed to be an ego-booster for her. Unfortunately for her, no one wanted to join her team. Her reputation preceded her.

"She built her team by cajoling and threatening, mainly co-workers, former co-workers and former husbands. No one really wanted to be there. I couldn't leave unless she approved. If I did, repayment of the outstanding balance of the loan plus a twenty-five percent fee was due immediately. That wasn't in the cards in the immediate future. I've been overextended ever since I bought more equipment and took on additional staff."

"Must be a bit of an inconvenience having to give up half of each Saturday to pickleball when it's a key day for landscaping," Rex said.

Brecken snorted. "You think?"

"Did you ask your former wife to let you off without the penalty?" Marla asked.

Brecken glanced away. "Yeah. A couple times."

"How recently?" Rex asked.

"A month ago."

"Since you were still there this past Saturday, apparently she continued to refuse you," Rex said.

"I've been hoping she'd tire of this whole idea of pickleball ever since she first got interested, especially since our team only wins on occasion. I don't think she much cared whether she and I won our games or not. She got a certain devilish satisfaction in bossing me around on the court. And the more she put down my performance, the more I messed up, even though I knew that part was taking a toll on her ego."

What a sick situation.

"What happened this past Saturday?" Marla asked. "Did you and your ex-wife have words before the game even started?"

He blinked. "No."

"Really?" Rex asked. "We've heard otherwise."

Brecken jerked his head. "You heard wrong." He switched his attention back to Marla. "Wait a sec. You were there Saturday. Giving out water, right?"

No way to duck that one, but she didn't need to expound on it. "Yes."

"Are you the one who said my ex and I were fighting?" His tone had become accusatory.

Rex answered for her. "Ms. Dane was there, and she's filled me in on what she observed. But there was another witness to you having words with Mrs. Wallace. I'm not at liberty to disclose who."

"Don't I have a right to face my accuser?"

"If your role in your ex-wife's murder ever goes to court, yes, you do. But not now while we're gathering preliminary information."

"Does this woman have an official role in your investigation?" Brecken asked. "Isn't that a conflict of interest? She's every bit a suspect as I am."

"Neither of you is deemed a suspect at this point," Rex replied evenly. "How about taking another shot at that question. What were you and your ex-wife arguing about last Saturday?"

Brecken studied his hands for several beats. "I wanted her to consider bringing Grace back on board."

"Why were you getting involved?" Marla asked. She hadn't noticed the two having anything to do with each other at the match, but then, they played at different times.

"Grace and I are old friends. She's had a tough time since Eloise bought out her share of the business. Not financially. Just getting her bearings careerwise. I asked Eloise to consider hiring her back as a consultant. She laughed in my face. She could be very cruel at times, especially since Grace was the original owner of the business."

Giving up her business to a woman like Eloise might be a powerful motive for murder. Might. They still had some questions for Brecken, but Grace should probably be the next person they interviewed.

"Tell us a little more about your friendship with Grace Adamson," she said.

"Like I said, we were old friends." He said it matter-of-factly. "You'll probably be talking to her, if you haven't already. Ask her about our friendship. Purely platonic."

Up until those last two words, she believed him. Why had he felt it necessary to couch his relationship with Grace in those terms?

"Did you notice anything unusual about your ex-wife on Saturday?" Rex asked.

"Other than her agitation level was slightly higher than usual, no."

"How about her water consumption?" Rex continued. "Did you observe her drinking from her water bottle at any time that morning?"

Brecken's forehead crinkled in thought. "I suppose so. All of us drink whenever we get a chance. That game takes a lot out of you. But I don't remember specifically seeing her take a swig."

"Do you recall what her water bottle looks like?" Rex asked.

"Is that important?" Brecken asked. "Was there something in her water?"

"Sorry, can't answer that," Rex replied. "Just reply to my question, if you will."

"Her bottle's ugly, olive green like the team colors she personally selected."

Marla and Rex exchanged looks. Was the fact that the ex knew the color of the victim's water bottle significant? Maybe. Time to move on.

Marla took the lead. "You said your ex-wife didn't have any siblings. What about other relatives?"

Brecken shook his head. "Her parents passed years ago. There may be a cousin or two somewhere, but she never mentioned them. If you're getting at her beneficiaries, I couldn't tell you. Her personal lawyer is Boris Doppler in Eagan. Check with him about her will. At one time I was the main beneficiary, but that changed with the divorce."

"Speaking of the divorce," Marla said, "how did that come about? Was it her idea or yours?"

The stare Brecken returned suggested he couldn't believe she had the gall to ask such a personal question. "It was a mutual decision. She'd gotten so engrossed in the business, there was little time for me."

"Was that before or after she purchased the business from Grace Adamson?" Rex asked. "We can check the court records, but you can make that easier for us."

"She bought out Grace about four years ago. Our divorce came two years earlier. Why is that important?"

"It's hard to say at this point," Rex responded. "For now, we're just gathering information about everyone who was close to her."

Brecken came to his feet. "No one was close to her! As far as friendship or other feelings were concerned. Her incessant self-centeredness has driven away anyone who might've been close to her at one time."

"In other words, her death doesn't bother you," Marla said. Rex would probably lecture her later about her lack of sympathy for the man, but she wanted to see how Brecken would react to her putting what appeared to be his real feelings out there.

"Not bothered by her death? Right now I'm more numb than anything else. If I wasn't the one handling the final details of her body once the medical examiner releases it, I might be able to relax, relieved this long nightmare is over."

Marla and Rex let that remark hang in the air before saying anything further.

Brecken appeared to realize the significance of his last statement. "That doesn't mean I killed her."

Rex paused another beat before speaking. "If you didn't murder your ex-wife, who do you think did?"

He didn't ask "if" Brecken knew who might have killed her but came right out and asked "who."

Brecken didn't hesitate to reply. "I have no idea. And if I did, I doubt I'd share that information with you. Whoever did the deed must have reached the end of their rope with her and ended their misery."

"Sorry you feel that way," Rex told him. "Your wife may have made life miserable for a lot of people, but killing her was still against the law."

"What will happen now with the outstanding portion of her loan to you?" Marla asked.

He blinked. "I have no idea. Depends on whatever she worked out with her attorney."

Marla didn't leave it there. "Is there a clause in the loan contract that forgives the outstanding balance if one of you dies?"

"You're kidding? That would've been an open invitation to kill her. Eloise was smarter than that. So you can eliminate that as my motive," Brecken replied.

"Nonetheless," Rex said, "please provide us with a copy of that document."

Brecken opened his mouth but closed it. "Are we done here?" Brecken asked instead, moving to his door instead of responding to Rex's last comment. "I've told you as much as I can remember about last Saturday and my relationship with Eloise."

Rex handed him his card. "We're just getting started with our investigation. We may be back. In the meantime, please contact me if anything else occurs to you."

Rex started his SUV immediately once they were back in it. "I need to put some distance between Brecken Wallace and us. It's too early for dinner, but how about some coffee? There are some nice cafes in this part of town."

"Good idea. This time, it's your turn to summarize our inter-view first."

eight

. . .

"You asked for my take on Brecken Wallace," Rex said once they were seated at a cozy booth near the back of a small café in West St. Paul. "I've got mixed feelings that need time to coalesce. I don't get how he could remain such an active part of his ex's life when he made no bones about not liking her. I'm divorced, and I still get along with my ex, but that doesn't mean I stay involved in her life."

"There's nothing *mixed* about that," she said.

"There's more. It's one thing that she still had some kind of hold over him this long after their divorce, but I didn't hear anything that suggested a strong motive for getting rid of her."

"You don't think he's a strong suspect?" she asked.

"Hard to say at this point. But there's a lot more to that guy than we got today. We have more digging to do." He took a sip from his coffee cup. The man liked his black. "Your turn. Do you agree with my initial assessment?"

"I agree about needing to know more about him to explain why he was still involved in her life. It seemed strange to me that he'd be the one making all the arrangements for her funeral or whatever they decide to do. Surely there was someone in her company, like her assistant, Tanner, who would've been in a better position to make those kinds of decisions. Maybe we can learn more about that by talking to her lawyer."

"Good thought. Let's talk to him next."

BORIS DOPPLER WAS part of a three-person practice located in a multiplex office building in Eagan. "I debated whether to make the Maple Knolls Police Department aware I am Eloise Wallace's attorney or wait until her death was determined to be murder," he told them as soon as they were seated in his office. "My current heavy caseload won out." He folded his hands and reclined in his leather armchair. "But you're here now, and I'll be happy to share what I can with you."

"We want to know about her will," Rex began. "Who inherits the business and her estate?"

"The will still has to be probated, but I can share the main details with you. Until she bought out Springboard Concepts from her then partner, Grace Adamson, Grace was to receive half the proceeds. Her husband, Brecken, was to receive the other half. Once Eloise owned the entire company, Grace was removed as a beneficiary. Her husband became the sole beneficiary, even after the divorce. He was removed from that position about two years ago when she named a Chloe Reardon as her sole beneficiary."

A new name that hadn't surfaced until now. "Chloe Reardon?" Marla asked. "Who is she?"

"I can't help you there," Doppler replied, "although I have a local address for the woman. I'll be informing her and having her sign the necessary papers once the will has cleared probate."

"Didn't you ask Mrs. Wallace why the change and who this woman was when she made the change?" Rex asked.

"Yes, of course I did. All Eloise would say was that she was a *friend of the family.*"

"Did she ever discuss a succession plan for the business in case something happened to her?" Marla asked.

"Succession plan?" Doppler replied, surprised by the question. "Eloise thought she was going to live forever. She only has a will because I insisted, if she wanted me to continue representing her."

"But surely she made some arrangement for the business to carry on if she was no longer able to be in charge?" Marla continued.

"Perhaps her assistant can answer that one, although I wouldn't be surprised if she left them high and dry."

Rex wasn't ready to give up just yet. "Did she leave the name of her next of kin?"

Doppler shook his head. "Her ex already called me about that because the funeral home had contacted him about her arrangements. I'll tell you what I told him, which is, no, she had me remove his name when they divorced, but she never provided another."

"Is that typical?" Marla asked, remembering how she'd updated her own "next of kin" data years before, after Carson died, when she placed Kitty's name there instead.

"Typical? No, but not unheard of. Keep in mind, a lot of folks don't even have a will. It's not like I didn't try to get her to give me a name or two, but she kept dodging the issue."

There didn't appear to be any more information they could glean from the man, so they thanked him and left.

"I'm liking that woman less and less," Marla said.

"Because she thought she was eternal?" Rex asked. "That was probably part of her drive as a businesswoman. She certainly wasn't much of a planner."

"Our visit with Doppler did net us another name. Chloe Reardon."

"I take it she wasn't there at the game or you would've mentioned her."

"She might've been sitting on the sidelines away from my water station. There were a few people there, but no one else approached me."

"Want to talk to her next?" Rex asked.

"How about meeting with the assistant first?" she replied. "I'd like to get the skinny on Chloe from someone else first before meeting her."

Rex called the number Tanner had given the first officer on the scene and discovered the young man was at home in St. Paul. He lived in a garage apartment in the older part of the town.

"Essy is closed indefinitely until it's determined who'll take charge from here on," he told them after they took seats in his tiny living room.

"Who will do that?" Rex asked.

"I don't know. If Nell was still there, she might know. Have you talked to her yet?"

"We'll be getting to her soon." Rex wasn't keen on revealing information about their investigation unless it worked to their benefit, but this time he apparently made an exception.

"Maybe Grace will come back, although she no longer owns Essy," Tanner said.

Was Tanner deliberately attempting to draw attention away from himself, despite his supposedly welcoming demeanor? "How about we talk about you right now and your relationship to the victim," Marla said. Out of the side of her eye, she caught a fleeting smile coming from Rex.

"Oh, sure. What do you want to know?" Tanner replied, settling back in his chair, even crossing his ankles.

"Tell us about last Saturday at the pickleball game," Rex said.

"Actually, it was a match. Three. Each game is played to eleven points. Two games of three win the match."

"Thank you. You were seen observing an argument between Mrs. Wallace and Nell Hampton and then talking to Mrs. Wallace yourself after Nell left the court. Tell us what that was all about," Rex said.

Tanner rubbed one pants leg with his hand. "That was nothing."

"What kind of *nothing*?" Rex pressed.

Tanner now stared at his hands rather than look either Rex or Marla in the eye. "Nell was the Essy accountant until a few weeks ago. She and Eloise had been arguing about the company's finances long before Eloise fired her. Neither would tell me about the final straw, but my guess is that it concerned use of Essy funds to underwrite an apartment for the use of staff."

"An apartment? What kind of use?" Rex asked.

"Eloise wasn't one for sharing details like that with me. What I learned about the situation came from some of the papers involved and calls she received from a rental agent in town."

And from whatever he could pick up from his eavesdropping, Marla suspected.

"Was the apartment for Mrs. Wallace?" she asked.

Tanner shook his head. "I don't think so, unless she was planning to sell her house and move closer to town."

"Then who was it for?" Marla pursued.

Their host pursed his lips as if debating how much to say and how much he could keep to himself. "The purchase agreement named Eloise as the owner."

His hesitation was telling. He knew who was to live there, and he didn't want to tell them.

Rex went into official mode. "We'll be going through all Mrs.

Wallace's papers, both personal and professional. We'll find out eventually. You could save this investigation precious time by telling us now. You do want to find her killer, don't you?"

Tanner was quick to reply. "Of course! I, uh, just don't want to confuse things by telling you what I suspect versus whatever the real facts are."

"That's very laudable, Mr. Oliver," Rex replied. "But that's our job, to sift through speculation and fact. Who was the apartment for?"

"Speculation, good word," Tanner said, shifting position. "As long as we call it that. Chloe. I think it was for Chloe Reardon."

Though the name had come up already in this investigation, Marla let him think this was a new name to them. "Who is she?"

Tanner grunted. "Eloise introduced her as 'a friend of the family' when she first came on board as an intern. She immediately assigned Chloe some of my work. Not anything big or important. Not then, anyhow. Later on, when she was hired full-time, I never saw an official employment application nor a job description for her. She was just there, taking on whatever tasks came her way with a smile. Always smiling." He looked at them directly. "No one smiles all the time."

They appeared to have opened a wound. This was unexpected but something they should follow up on. "What are you telling us?" she asked. "That you don't like her? That you don't trust her?" Or maybe he was jealous of this newcomer.

"I was never Eloise's partner or confidante. But we got along pretty well. I got her. I accepted her autocratic ways once I learned how to work around them. But that changed once Chloe was on the scene. Eloise turned over more and more of my responsibilities to her without replacing them with even more important duties for me."

"Were you jealous of her?" Rex asked, coming right out with the question.

"Suspicious. I watched her 'working' Eloise. She rarely came right out and asked for anything. No, I'd respect someone who acknowledged what she wanted and worked to get it. But Chloe isn't straightforward like that. She hints around about things, plants ideas with others and then acts surprised when they follow through. She's ... devious. There, I said it."

Time to go for the kill. "It's interesting, Tanner, because some of those we've talked to have said or inferred the same about you and your rise in the company," Marla said. It was only a half-truth based more on what Liz and Brecken hadn't said about him than their outright observations.

Tanner leaned forward. "If you're trying to bait me, it won't work. I know full well how I'm viewed by others. There are times when I don't like myself very much either. But I made a choice when I first started working for Eloise. I could either be liked by others or get ahead by doing anything Eloise wanted. But I've been honest about my career-climbing ambitions. Chloe is different. She's a manipulator."

"Some might characterize your boss that way," Marla pointed out.

He shook his head vigorously. "No, that wasn't the case, at least during the time I've known her. Manipulators work behind the scenes to get what they want. Eloise was out there with her demands. She was strong-willed, combative and relentless in getting them."

The next few questions were a repeat of what they'd asked Brecken about seeing anything out of the ordinary concerning Eloise's water bottle.

"Did you go through her equipment bag?" Tanner asked as his response. "If you had, you'd have noticed that she carried a second water bottle. Even though she was the one who insisted the team have a water person, she preferred to supply all of her own water"

Marla resisted the urge to check out Rex's reaction to that new item. Who had missed that one?

They got the name of the brand, and then Rex asked the final question. "Who do you think killed your boss?"

Tanner considered. "You've probably run into more than one person with a strong motive for getting rid of Eloise, and you'll probably find more. But who'd take the risk? The benefit of removing her from the scene isn't as strong as the payback. I don't know who would take that risk."

Very telling statement, unless Tanner was deliberately trying to mislead them. Marla's assessment of the man had changed during this interview. How remained to be seen.

nine

. . .

"That went differently than I anticipated," Marla told Rex when they were once again in his SUV headed back to the condo complex.

"In what way?" Rex replied, his attention on the late-afternoon traffic.

"My first impression of him at the pickleball match was that of a hanger-on, a gofer who lived for pleasing his boss."

"That pretty well describes the guy we just interviewed. What was different for you?"

"He realizes that's how he comes across and doesn't apologize for it. He's more than just a lackey."

"More like a jealous lackey?" Rex asked, shooting her a grin.

"He explained the jealous part, and for now I believe him," Marla replied. "Plus, Chloe has become even more interesting."

"You don't think he was intentionally trying to throw us off him as a suspect?"

She considered his question. "Anything's possible at this point. But coupled with what we learned from the attorney, Chloe has moved up on my list of potential suspects."

"We're down to her, Grace and Nell. Do you want to keep going today?"

"I want to appease my curiosity about Chloe as soon as possible," she replied.

Chloe was not at the address Doppler had given them, but her roommate, a tall, skinny redhead who identified herself as Daria Powers, was able to provide a forwarding address. "Moved out overnight with no advance notice. At least she was up-to-date on her share of the rent," Powers said.

"Besides that, what can you tell us about Ms. Reardon?" Rex asked.

She shrugged. "She wasn't here that much. Came in around eleven most nights and left around eight in the morning. Sometimes she stayed out all night. She was neat, one good thing about her. Cleaned up after herself, did her laundry regularly."

"Was there a boyfriend or otherwise?" Marla asked.

"No one she brought here or talked to on the phone."

"Friendly?" Rex asked.

"Enough, not that we shared any confidences," Powers replied.

"Anything else you can tell us about her?" Marla asked.

Powers leaned against the doorframe. "Yeah, now that I think about it. She lived here not quite a year. When she first arrived, she tended to wear jeans and T-shirts. By the time she left, her wardrobe included skirts, jackets and blouses. Business wear, you know?"

They thanked her for her information and set off for the new address she'd given them.

This new location was more upscale than the older building they'd just visited. The apartment was on the third floor, reached by elevator. They rang several times before someone came to the door. A young woman, about five six with long blond hair and the lightest of blue eyes, answered.

"We're here to see Chloe Reardon," Rex said. "Is that you?"

"Yes," she answered pleasantly.

Rex did the introductions and asked if they could enter. She showed them to a living room done in ivory and tan. The furniture was new and looked expensive, but there didn't appear to be any personal touches in the room like photos or accessories, although one tall green plant took place of honor in a corner.

"I can't tell you much about poor Eloise," she said before they'd asked any questions. "I only worked with her the last few years."

"Tell us what you do know," Marla said, leaving the question open for now to hear what the young woman would volunteer about her former boss.

"She was like a mentor to me, open, encouraging, willing to show me the ropes in the PR business. Her death came as a shock."

"You got along with her?" Rex asked.

She tilted her head and offered a curious smile. "Yes, of course. Why do you ask?"

"Others who knew her haven't been quite as positive about their relations with her," Marla replied.

She dismissed the statement with a shrug. "Others didn't understand her. She was a driven woman, single-minded about her future. Sometimes her decisions got in the way of others' plans."

Rex ran a hand along the arm of the overstuffed chair in which he was seated. "Nice place."

"Thank you. I like it, too."

"You just moved here recently, we understand," Rex continued.

"About three weeks ago, yes."

"Can you afford it?" he asked, getting to the point.

She blinked. "Ah, you heard about that arrangement."

"Arrangement?" Marla asked. Surely the dead woman hadn't been "keeping" her?

Chloe waved her question away. "This place is fully furnished. I'm a sort of on-site housekeeper. I keep things in shape for when out-of-town clients are in town, when I make myself scarce so Eloise can ... could entertain them. In return, I don't pay rent or utilities, although I do pay for my own groceries and am expected to stock the bar and fridge when there are guests."

"We see," Rex said, although Marla wasn't sure she did. It sounded too good to be true. Then he went on to the obvious. "What'll happen now that she's no longer around?"

She offered a disarming smile. "I assume the arrangement will continue with whoever takes over Essy."

"Do you know who'll take over the company?" Marla asked, even though no one else seemed to know.

"I, uh, well, no, not exactly. Eloise and I had been discussing me acting as her backup so she could spend more time traveling and visiting clients, but I'm not sure I could handle everything right away. Tanner probably thinks he should take over, but Eloise never planned that for him or for Essy. He's a hard worker, but he lacks the vision to run it."

Interesting take on Eloise's former right-hand man. Clearly, the dead woman had been filling Chloe's head with big dreams. Had she seriously thought Chloe could take over for her someday? Marla couldn't wait to hear Grace and Nell's side of this story.

"If you and Eloise Wallace were so close, why weren't you on the pickleball team?" Rex asked.

"I was a substitute. I was unable to be there last Saturday."

"Oh, why was that?" Marla asked, more out of curiosity than as a true follow-up to Chloe's statement.

The young woman's demeanor changed immediately. "Do I have to answer that?"

"Withholding information may only raise our doubts about your credibility," Rex said.

"It doesn't have any bearing on Eloise's murder."

"Why don't you let us decide that," Rex told her.

She bit a lip and let her gaze wander everywhere in the room except toward them. "Can you guarantee confidentiality?" she asked.

"I'm sorry, no," Rex replied, maintaining a firm tone. "We can't guarantee we can keep whatever you tell us between just us, but if it's not pertinent to solving this murder, maybe we won't have to share whatever you tell us with anyone else."

She released a sigh. "I've been taking a gourmet cooking class. It's offered on Saturdays by this noted chef. She's here on weekends only because she spends weekdays in New York."

Gourmet cooking. Not at all what Marla had been expecting, although she couldn't say what she had been anticipating. Chloe was attempting to come across as friendly and welcoming. An open book. And yet ...? The more they learned from her, the weirder Marla's vibes got.

"Gourmet cooking," she repeated. "Do you have hopes of becoming a chef someday?"

"Oh, no," Chloe quickly replied. "I'm happy in the PR business. Actually, it was Eloise who suggested I might enjoy taking this class. She met the chef on one of her business trips to New York."

"Did she realize the class would conflict with pickleball?" Rex asked, apparently as curious as Marla why the dead woman would be willing to forfeit someone who could have added to the team.

"Oh, yes. She wasn't thrilled about the schedule, but she thought it was important enough for her to spare me."

"Why was that?" Marla asked.

Chloe's blue eyes went wide. "She never said as much, but for some time it felt like she was grooming me to someday take her place. Even though gourmet cooking wasn't one of her strengths, she thought it would help me better navigate the corporate world."

"How's it coming?" Rex asked.

Their interviewee clasped her hands together. "I'm not ready to prepare a top-notch meal for you yet, if that's what you mean. But I have learned some techniques I never knew existed in my open-a-can-or-a-box cooking style."

"Why do you want to keep this class confidential?" Rex asked.

She chuckled. "I guess that did appear a little melodramatic. The thing is, Eloise didn't want anyone else at Essy to know. Or her ex or ex-partner, Grace. Even now that she's ... gone ... I feel I should respect her feelings."

"Since you weren't at the pickleball game on Saturday, when was the last time you saw Mrs. Wallace?" Marla asked, deciding they'd heard enough about the secret cooking class for now.

"I last saw her on Friday afternoon. I stopped by her office to wish her and the team well the next day."

"How would you describe her mood?"

"Preoccupied. With work, that is. But that was typical. She was also pumped about the match the next day."

"How did she seem physically?" Rex asked.

"You mean did she appear ill? No. She seemed agitated, but that was par for the course. She always had several things going and on her mind at once." She paused, as if debating if she should say more.

"Yes?" Rex asked, prodding her along.

"I texted her Saturday night to check on the outcome of the

match. Her return text was brief, not like her. Somewhat disjointed, but I interpreted that as disappointment at their losses. Do you think—should I have paid more attention?" She wrung her clasped hands. "Maybe if I had, we'd have caught whatever was ailing her and she'd still be alive." Her last words were almost a whine.

"But since you didn't follow up, we assume you weren't concerned about the abbreviated text," Marla said, making sure they correctly understood what she'd just told them. Thus far, it was the closest contact anyone had with the victim before her death.

Chloe stopped wringing her hands long enough to pull at the collar of her knit top. "No, I wasn't concerned, or I definitely would have gotten back to her. Even gone to her house."

"Could we see that text?" Rex asked.

"Uh, no. Sorry. Unless a text is absolutely necessary to retain, I delete everything as soon as I've read it."

The police could probably recover it, if Goodhue thought it essential. "Can you recall what it said?" Marla asked.

"Not word for word, but the gist of it was that they'd won one match and put up a good fight in the other two. What she actually wrote was shorter."

"She didn't mention feeling off or otherwise woozy or sick?" Rex asked.

"No! If she had, I would've gone to her immediately. She lives —lived alone. I knew there wouldn't be anyone there to take care of her."

"She wasn't seeing anyone?" Marla asked.

"Personally? No, at least not that I'm aware of. But Eloise kept a lot to herself. There may have been someone no one knew about."

They'd come to the end of their questions for the time being. Rex gave her his card and said his thing about contacting them if she remembered anything else. They left the apartment and headed for his SUV.

"Let's go to my condo and go over everything we've learned today," Rex said. "My head is buzzing."

"Isn't that normal?" she returned.

"To a degree. But while we've been getting pretty much the same take on the woman from everyone we've talked to, everyone has had a different reason for that opinion."

"And we still have two key witnesses to interview," she reminded him. "Do we need to get their viewpoints tonight before anyone has a chance to compare notes?"

"If they felt the need to cover each other's tracks, they would've done so by now," Rex replied. "They had all of yesterday to contact each other before we got started today."

"Then we hold off on Grace and Nell until tomorrow."

"Yeah. If I hadn't made it a habit not to drink while investigating a case, I could use something really strong right now. Since that's not in the cards, I'll pig out on pizza instead."

ten

. . .

*A*s they neared the condo building, Marla received a frantic text from Kitty.

Help! Take a break from crime-busting to save my life!

She read the text to Rex.

"Is she serious?" he asked.

"I have no idea. It could be anything from a broken nail to a trip to the hospital with Kitty. Can we postpone our discussion long enough for me to check on her?"

"Sure. I'll even come with you in case she needs my help too."

Kitty met them in the kitchen, where she was staring at some of the same ingredients Marla had used for making the apple pies. "Thank goodness you were able to break away from tracking down the killer. I need you here right now."

"I don't see any blood," Marla replied.

"And you're standing upright," Rex added.

"How are we supposed to save your life?" Marla asked.

"I need to bake an apple pie by seven thirty," she responded, motioning toward the items lining the island. "Or rather, you need to bake one, with me helping enough to claim ownership."

"That's the emergency?" She wasn't surprised, just a little irritated. She'd been through Kitty's so-called emergencies more than once before.

"It is to me," Kitty said, running a hand through her hair. "Somehow Hub got the idea I was an excellent pie baker." She turned to Rex. "That's Hub Sherman, the guy I'm currently seeing socially."

Marla knew exactly how Hub got the wrong idea about Kitty's baking skills, but more to the point, why hadn't Kitty set him straight? Surely that wouldn't have ended their relationship. Baking another pie might be just the kind of break she needed right now but not before she gave Kitty grief for interrupting their investigation. "You want Rex and me to put our investigation on hold to help you impress your boyfriend? To seemingly save you from once again skating over the truth?"

"Uh, yes. You're here now, and it won't take long. Especially because this pie has to bake and cool in the next two and a half hours." Her jaunty tone hadn't changed one bit after Marla's questions.

Although she knew she'd cave eventually, Marla wasn't about to help Kitty until she let her know her request was ill-timed. "We've had a full day talking to people associated with the victim, and our heads are full. We were just about to have a bite to eat at Rex's condo and rehash what we've learned. Baking a pie might throw us off."

Kitty got that look on her face, the one where she lit up like she'd just had the brightest of ideas. "On the contrary, this little break is exactly what you need for all that info to gel so you can go back to it later and examine it in a clear light."

Kitty wasn't one to admit defeat. Instead, she invented ways to get herself out of or around the scrapes she created. This was one of those times.

Before Marla could hassle Kitty further, Rex came to Kitty's aid. "Can I help? I know a little about how to bake a pie. My grandmother taught me. Haven't made one in years, though."

So much for chastising Kitty further. "Okay. We'd better get started if this pie is going to get baked and cool in this short span of time we have," Marla said.

"Thank you, guys! I'll be in your debt. I've already peeled and quartered the apples for the filling to save us time," Kitty gushed.

"The ones I'd put aside to make an apple crisp," Marla said. *Goodbye to that plan.*

"That woman getting herself murdered has put that project on hold indefinitely," Kitty said. "They would've spoiled waiting for you to solve the case."

So much for Kitty's confidence in their investigative talents.

"What kind are they?" Rex asked.

"Honeycrisp," Kitty replied. "That's all our mom used when she could get them. Granny Smith are a little too tart for me, even with added sugar."

Rex nodded his approval. "Good choice. Why don't you add the other ingredients to the apples, Kitty, while we get the rest of the crust ready?"

Since all Kitty had to do was prepare sugar, cinnamon and a touch of nutmeg to sprinkle over the apples, she agreed to take on that task. Marla and Rex headed to the island for the main event.

Marla gathered flour, shortening, salt and a cup of cold water. After she'd measured out the flour, she began to cut in the shortening with a pastry cutter.

"Wait. That's how you mix the ingredients?" Rex asked.

Marla held up the pastry cutter. "With this, yes. I had to order one online when I made some pies for Kitty last week. Our mom always used one, but Kitty's stock of kitchen equipment is sadly lacking."

"That's because I rarely do any baking, which is why you two are helping me now," Kitty said from the sidelines.

"You don't have a food processor?" Rex asked.

"I have a blender I never use in the pantry. Will that work?" Kitty replied.

"Maybe." He shot a look at the assembled ingredients. "Where's the butter?"

"I tried adding butter a few times a while back when I was baking pies more often," Marla said. "My crusts browned too fast. One even burned. So I stopped using it."

"Was it at room temp or still refrigerated?" he asked.

She thought back. That was a long time ago, right after she and Carson had first been married. "I'd just assembled all my ingredients. But the butter may have softened a tad by the time I added it."

"Did you cut it up before adding it?"

What was with all the questions? "Rex, you're not interviewing suspects right now. Yes, I cut it up so I could mix it with the shortening."

"You mixed the two together before cutting them into the flour and salt?"

"That seemed to make sense."

Rex hesitated, as if weighing whether to say something more or just get on with prepping Kitty's masterpiece.

"Go on. What aren't you saying?" Marla asked. Whatever it was would come out sooner or later. Might as well deal with it now.

"Since you asked ... I dice the butter into small pats and then douse it with some of the flour before mixing them in. That's after I've combined most of the flour and all of the salt and shortening in a food processor. After that, I add the flour-coated butter. I started doing this after I read somewhere that the flour on the butter prevents the water from saturating the flour to form too much gluten. I guess you get a flakier crust with less gluten."

"Listen to you," Kitty said, admiring Rex's input. "You could easily be a pastry chef in some fancy restaurant."

"Hold off the praises until you've tasted the proof of my efforts," he replied. "That is, if your sister wants to try some of my suggestions?"

Marla didn't know whether to be insulted by his input or relieved to have someone else assisting her. The two pies she'd made for Kitty's lesson turned out okay, but they hadn't been particularly tasty. "Okay, if you think her blender can substitute for a food processor?"

"Let's give it a try," he said.

He did the honors, mixing the ingredients per his recommendations. A lovely ball of dough resulted, which he divided in two.

"You need to chill them for at least an hour," Rex said. "Marla and I have to leave, so let's talk through your next steps. Do you have a pie crust mat?" he asked once the circular balls were in the fridge.

"No," Kitty replied. "I've never heard of such a thing."

"She does have parchment paper," Marla said. "I got a box at the grocery store when we bought the other ingredients."

"Okay, beats rolling it out on just a flat flour-covered surface," Rex said. He addressed Kitty. "I don't suppose you have a French-style rolling pin?"

Kitty gave Marla a pinched look, not tracking.

"I had one years ago," Marla said. "Kitty has the more conventional style. That was actually here when I checked her inventory."

"Guess you'll have to use that style then," he said, discouraged.

"What's so great about the French style?" Kitty asked.

"It has a smaller circumference, so it gives the rolled-out crust a smoother surface. The ends of the pin are flattened out, making it easier to hold on to," Marla said.

They all agreed on the need to flour the parchment paper and the rolling pin to keep the dough from sticking. "It will work best to roll the same direction," he said.

"Won't the crust become a longer strip rather than a round circle?" Marla asked.

"Not if you turn the parchment paper after each roll," he said. "How about a slider? Do you have one of those, Kitty?"

"I don't even know what one is," she replied.

"A long knife will probably work. You'll need it to keep the underside of the dough from sticking to the parchment paper," he told her.

"I've always kept the underside floured to prevent sticking," Marla said.

"You need that, too," he replied.

"I suppose you have tips on making the perfect filling too," Marla said, trying to keep her tone from sounding sarcastic, because so far he had produced what looked like pretty good crusts. Maybe not world-class, but then, he didn't have all the tools he needed.

"Can't help you there. My granny was very particular about her fruit fillings. I got to watch, but she never trusted me to handle them on my own."

Marla had to chuckle. "I'm trying to picture you letting your grandmother take charge."

"She knew what she wanted and how to get it. Her grandson was there to observe and learn. She was a great teacher."

"She must've been," Marla said. "I can see how you picked up on those traits."

"I'll take that as a compliment," he returned, refusing to be insulted.

"You're on your own for the rest of the process," Marla told Kitty, since this pie-baking lesson had already cut into her time to debrief with Rex.

"You're leaving me?" Kitty cried, panic underlying her tone.

"We did the hard part," Rex said. "Just roll out one crust at a time. Once you've placed your chopped-up apples in the bottom crust, do your thing sprinkling sugar, cinnamon and a touch of nutmeg. Let that sit out while you roll out the top crust and then bake. As easy as apple pie," he added with a sardonic smile.

"Take great care removing the pie from the oven on time," Marla told her sister as she and Rex prepared to leave.

Kitty put a hand over her chest. "I'm not a complete novice, Marla. I cooked for two kids and a picky husband for years. I just haven't done much cooking or baking since the kids moved out."

She was right. While Kitty had been fending for her family, Marla had counted on a cook and housekeeper so she could make films and later appear on TV. "What I meant," she attempted to explain, "was that you'll probably be getting ready for your date when it's time to take the pie out. Just set the oven timer and the one on your phone and you'll be fine. Send us a photo of the finished product and let us know about Hub's reaction."

"Will do. Thank you both. I've ordered a pizza to be delivered to Rex's condo in about five minutes as my small token of appreciation."

"It was actually a pleasure to take a break and relive some of my fonder memories from my boyhood," Rex told her.

Kitty turned to Marla. "The two of you worked well together.

Maybe you should get Rex to partner up with you on your video."

Marla groaned inwardly. They'd almost escaped without any more discussion of the ill-fated video.

Rex pivoted toward Marla. He lifted a brow. "That's right. I heard you were working on a video."

Marla attempted to wave it off. "I've just been playing around with the idea. "C'mon, let's go check on this pizza Kitty ordered for us."

eleven

. . .

Rex waited until they reached his condo before mentioning Marla's attempt to make a video. "So? You're gonna try it?" he asked.

Kitty knew Marla didn't want Rex to be aware of her plans yet. Still, she'd brought them up. Deliberately. It hadn't been a slip of the tongue. Despite the fact that they were deeply embroiled in the Wallace investigation, Kitty thought her sister should be getting on with this new venture. What better way to do so than to get Rex involved? As demonstrated with the pie, he wasn't one to hold back.

"Kitty got ahead of herself. We tried it once, and it didn't go well."

"What happened?"

She tried to steer clear of the subject. "It was no big deal."

"Really? Marla Danes, who certainly knows her stuff in front of the camera, had problems with a video? Why didn't you go with the idea of a podcast like I suggested to you in the first place? That would've been a natural transition for you."

"Can we just drop it?" she said. "We have so much to discuss about today's interviews."

He studied her a moment. "If that's the way you want it, Marla, but I don't understand. Either podcasting or videocasting seem perfect for you. At least while you're waiting for the right part to come along."

She didn't reply to his comment. "Okay if I spread out on the sectional while we wait for the pizza to arrive? Maybe we can cover one or two of the interviews."

He waited for her to relax on one side of the sectional, then settled in one of the overstuffed easy chairs. "We've already decided that Liz is probably not the killer, even though she didn't care one bit for the woman. She says she remained on the team in hopes Eloise would help promote her fashion line. But as open as she appeared to be with us, we came away from her interview thinking she wasn't sharing everything."

"So we talk to her again, but only after we've learned more from the others than we uncovered today," she said. "Next up, Brecken Wallace. We've already agreed he's holding back. He certainly steered his way around suggesting a possible killer." Another thought hit her. "It's kind of sad, actually. The fact that there's no one else to deal with her remains. No apparent relatives, no children, no friends. I wonder how much he's enjoying the task of decision-maker."

"Why do you say that?"

"It's sort of his opportunity to have the last say, since she didn't leave any instructions. He could make selections he knows would upset her if she were still around. You know, no funeral, just a memorial service. Cremation versus burial. No eulogies. Music she hated. Those sorts of things."

He gave her a strange look. "You have an evil mind, Marla. Remind me not to let you handle my final details."

"I was just speculating. For such a seemingly smart woman, it's not easy to believe she never thought about her death. Or a succession plan for Essy."

"Anything else about the ex-husband?" he asked.

"His relationship with Grace needs more light. He said it was just platonic and even suggested we talk to her about it, but by the time we get to her tomorrow, he probably will have contacted her and given her the party line."

"Yeah, we missed a beat there, not telling him to keep what he told us to himself. But maybe that will work in our favor," Rex said.

"How so?"

"If what she tells us sounds like a repeat of what he told us, we'll know there's a closer tie between them than he wanted us to believe," Rex replied. "Any other points about Brecken?"

She thought back through their interview. "He seemed to be totally oblivious to how much water she imbibed during the morning. That might make sense if he hadn't been her partner and out there on the court with her. Have you seen those courts? There's not much room for moving around. I think he knows more about her hydration habits than he's telling us, although that may simply be because he didn't pay much attention."

"But Tanner knew about the equipment bag," Rex pointed out, "at least the fact that it contained two water bottles and were filled with her own special spring water."

"Someone could've brought an identical bottle filled with poison and swapped it without her or anyone else knowing, if no one saw them making the switch."

"That's a big IF," he replied. "But it is a plausible explanation."

"I wish we knew more about the tox results."

"I'll check again with Goodhue," Rex said, "but he would've let us know as soon as he knew anything."

"We learned a lot more from Tanner," she went on. "He definitely doesn't like Chloe, and even though he denies being jealous of her relationship with Eloise, he didn't like being replaced as the woman's closest confidante."

"Then there's Chloe Reardon herself," he said. "Interesting subject to say the least. She wants to come across as helpful, the perfect assistant. But it felt like she was trying too hard."

"I knew actors like her. Usually newcomers, like Chloe, who were trying to get ahead faster than their talents and experience would allow. Some were quite obvious in their efforts, but a few hid their motivation too well. People who trusted them got burned."

"Did that ever happen to you?"

She took a moment to reflect on her dealings with other actors over the years. "Are you familiar with the movie *All About Eve*? Probably not. It came out in the 1950s. A young woman becomes the personal assistant of a famous actress and insinuates herself so much into the woman's life she starts to become her. Every so often, a younger actress who was guest-starring on the show started showing signs of something like that with me. Unless you're overly cynical and skeptical of anyone showing positive interest in you, you don't notice their overtures at first. You accept them as honest admiration or the desire to learn from you. Once I spotted the tendency, I had to be careful not to come across too strongly or I'd get the reputation as a shrew."

He steepled his fingers under his chin and studied her.

"What?" she asked, picking up on his change of mood.

"I'm trying to picture you in that role. When you first arrived and even when we first found ourselves working together, I saw you as this 'Hollywood type,' haughty and demanding, but I soon learned I'd stuck you with my idea of a big-time actress. That was unfair. I hope by now I've shown you how wrong I was."

Though she'd come to know Rex as a straight shooter when speaking his mind was concerned, he didn't often bare his personal feelings like this. Though humbled by his admission, she didn't want to embarrass him with her own feelings. *Keep it simple, Marla.* "Thanks, Rex. I wasn't sure how partnering with you would work, but I've been pleasantly surprised."

"Yeah, well, uh, back to Chloe. I was getting so many different vibes from that young woman, I want to make sure I don't forget any."

"Okay, what else did you get from her?" she asked, happy to shift away from the more personal turn their talk had taken.

"That whole free apartment thing has me wondering. All she had to do was keep it clean and fill the fridge when guests were on the way. Sounds too good to be true."

"That's what Tanner said the victim and the former accountant, Nell, were arguing about last Saturday."

Rex nodded, remembering. "In other words, she had some questions about the apartment too."

"It's not unheard of in the entertainment world to maintain a property for the use of guests," she said. "Lodging costs have increased so much in recent years, in some circles this tactic is viewed as one way to reduce expenses. But here in Minnesota, I don't know how common it is."

"The former roommate said the move happened overnight. That's curious, too."

"And where does she go when guests show up?" Marla said. "The old roomie didn't mention Chloe coming back there occasionally."

He narrowed his eyes, considering that comment. "Besides there being no rent, that is telling. Does it suggest anything shady to you?"

"Shady? That may not be the exact word I'm thinking of, but yes. It suggests that Eloise was not only grooming Chloe for more than just running the business someday, but she expected her to provide certain clients with sex when called for. Whether

Chloe was aware of her boss's intentions remains to be seen. And keep in mind, I said it *suggests*. I didn't say it *meant*."

"I get that, but think of it, Marla. If what we suspect was going on, we may have found the real motive for her murder."

"But Chloe must've realized what was going on," she said. "Why else would she have gone along with Eloise's suggestion she take that gourmet cooking course?"

"That course could be part of the plan. The 'hostess' entertains the guests with her culinary expertise."

Marla thought through the ramifications of the scenario. "We need to learn more about the health of the victim's business. If what we think might've been happening was the case, it could be that Eloise had some big plans in mind. Plans that included upping her catering to out-of-town clients. Clients who expected to be wined and dined and entertained in every sense of the word."

"Nell needs to be first on our list of interviews tomorrow," he said.

"Good place to end our first day's efforts," she said. "Want to return to Kitty's condo with me and see if there's any apple pie left?"

twelve

. . .

Nell agreed to meet them at her home in Maple Knolls at nine the next morning.

Rex had copied Marla on the brief summary of the day's findings he sent to Goodhue the night before. "You didn't mention much about Chloe Reardon," she said while he drove.

"I stuck with the facts, which were few. But it was enough to show the chief we were making progress. No need to get him speculating too."

"Thanks for reminding him, again, that we need the toxicology results in order to shape our questions."

"Given the way he checks in with us so frequently, I have no doubt he's doing the same with the lab," he replied. "Which is understandable, given how he's put his reputation on the line bringing two lay consultants on board."

"Sorry you didn't get to taste the apple pie last night because Kitty left it with Hub Sherman. I really wanted to check out how much flakier it was after using your ideas with the crust."

"We could always make another?" he said.

"You're teasing, right?" she replied.

"Mostly, although it was kinda fun putting something together from scratch again. We were a pretty good team."

"As long as I agreed with all your suggestions," she kidded back.

"Are you ready to talk about Kitty's comment that I should've been part of your attempt at a video?" he asked.

"No. She knew very well that I didn't want to discuss my disastrous attempt at a video with you and yet let it slip out. Her way of making me tell you about it. I hate when she does that to me."

"She thought she was helping, but if you really don't want to talk about it, I'll leave it alone. For now. Maybe once we've solved this case you'll be more amenable to talking about it."

"Thanks. We're almost at Nell's anyhow. Not enough time for a personal discussion," she replied.

They pulled up to the address Nell had given them. "Let's hope we make good progress with today's interviews."

Nell offered them coffee as soon as they arrived, which they declined but insisted she have. She showed them to her sun porch, where they each took a seat at a round table.

Appearing to be in her late thirties, Nell had attempted to pull her ash-blond hair into a loose ponytail, half of which was already escaping. She wore denim blue jeans and a long-sleeved, cotton plaid shirt with a dark stain on the front. Even though she knew they were coming, she didn't look like she was ready for visitors. What struck Marla the most about the woman's appearance was her pallor.

"If you weren't ready for us just yet, Ms. Hampton, we can come back a little later," Marla said, even though she was anxious to hear what Nell had to say about her former boss.

Nell swept away the offer. "No, you were right on time. I apologize for my appearance. My wife, Katharine, passed away six weeks ago after a long-term illness. We both knew this time would come and prepared for it, at least financially. But the emotional toll is so much more difficult than I ever imagined. I just can't seem to get myself together these days."

Of course. Liz had said something about the wife's passing, but with everything else she was learning about the people associated with Eloise Wallace, that information had gone to the back of her mind. It shouldn't have. Of all people, she should know how crippling the death of a loved one could be. "I've been there myself, Ms. Hampton. Years ago, but those feelings never go away altogether. They just get easier to live with."

"Thanks. Please call me Nell, if that's allowed."

"We'll stick with Ms. Hampton," Rex told her.

"Oh, sure." She relaxed her shoulders. "How can I help you?"

"Could you tell us why you were fired?" Marla asked, moving immediately to the key question.

Nell's eyes fluttered slightly, but she didn't protest. "I was fired over a disagreement I had with the owner over how money was being spent. I was the accountant for over ten years. I was hired by the previous owner, Grace Adamson, before Eloise even came on the scene. Grace and I had a good working relationship. We saw eye to eye about Essy's fiscal policy and actions. When Eloise became her partner, things began to change. I had a fiduciary responsibility to assure Essy's finances were handled correctly and expeditiously. That meant I sometimes had to say no. Certain items or actions either could not be afforded at that time or company funds couldn't be used for certain expenditures."

"How did Grace react when you had to say no?" Marla asked.

"Grace usually stepped in and found a compromise Eloise and I could agree to. But once Grace sold Essy to Eloise and Eloise was completely in charge, that changed. As long as she wasn't completely outside the law in her handling of finances, she thought she could get away with her decisions. You've probably already heard from others that she was ambitious and had big dreams for taking Essy to the next level.

"In the past few months, she talked of growing the company away from local business and focused more on the national scene. She'd even begun to talk about foreign business. I continued to protest several of her decisions, especially several expenditures she made while I was away on personal leave. She'd shifted some of my duties to Chloe Reardon, even though Chloe has no accounting background, saying someone had to keep up the financial part of Essy in my absence. I'd anticipated the day when I'd have to be gone and made arrangements for an accounting temp to handle those transactions that couldn't wait for my return. Eloise had the nerve to accuse me of spending more money than necessary when the tasks could be absorbed by current staff."

"What happened during the time you were on leave?" Rex asked.

"I could tell my days at Essy were numbered. Truthfully, my performance suffered the last few months, and a lot of that was due to my emotional state. But she didn't make it easy for me, either. I sensed but couldn't prove that she was deliberately setting me up to either resign in frustration or so she could fire me.

"The final straw was the apartment she purchased during my leave. Purchased, not leased. Even though I didn't agree it was a smart business move, had she leased it, we could've gotten out of it in time if it didn't work out. But a purchase would take considerable time, if ever, to show return on the investment. I probably went too far when I confronted her, accusing her of bad business practice that would ruin Essy. She fired me on the spot."

"Given that, why did you continue to play on the pickleball team?" Rex asked.

"Grace came to see me while I was still on leave and begged me to come back to the team so there'd be someone there she could get along with. I turned her down at first. It was only on the advice of my grief counselor that I reconsidered," Nell replied. "I never did understand Eloise's strong attachment to the sport. None of our players were all that good. We lost a lot of matches. And I don't think anyone other than Eloise wanted to be there. But for reasons that escape me, everyone stayed on."

"Tell us about the confrontation you had with her last Saturday before the games started," Marla said.

"You heard about that. I guess I started it. I'd run into Chloe at the grocery store the day before. If you've talked to her already, you probably know that she comes across as rather naive. Whether that's for real, I'm not sure. She was so excited she couldn't resist telling me about her new lodging and the great deal Eloise had offered her. I asked her several questions to clarify that I'd heard her correctly, that she wasn't having to pay for it. I kept my concerns to myself, but by the next day, I was seething at what I considered such a waste of money, and it all came to the forefront when Eloise walked on the court. I knew the timing and place were inappropriate for such a confrontation, but it all just spilled out."

"How did she react?" Marla asked.

"At first she was taken aback. She wasn't used to direct accusations. People tended to kowtow to her or complain about her behind her back. But it didn't take her long to regain stride. She told me her business was no longer any concern of mine and to keep out of it. She even accused me of having lost my sense of propriety in the wake of Katharine's death. And then she sort of settled down, like there was no issue at all. I was just acting crazy."

"But still, you stayed. You didn't walk off the court then and there?" Rex asked.

"Right. When I think back on my actions now, I can't believe I just took it. But that was the effect she had on people."

"Did you speak to her further the rest of the match?" Rex asked.

"Not outright, although I may have called out encouragement to her and Brecken while they were playing."

"How about any time after that?"

"No. I knew I'd said more than I should have already. She wasn't going to change her mind about the apartment."

They asked the same questions about the dead woman's water bottles. Nell hadn't noticed anyone near the bag and hadn't realized her former boss brought two bottles.

"Is there anything else you can tell us that might help our investigation?" Marla asked as they were winding down.

"You mean who do I think killed her? The woman certainly stepped on a lot of toes, but I can't think of anyone who would have been so offended by her actions they would murder her." She brought a hand to her chest. "Look at me. She fired me at a time when I was not emotionally equipped to deal with the loss of my job. But kill her over it? No. There's still enough of my mental and emotional maturity left to deal with my situation without getting violent. And if I wasn't ready to do it, I can't imagine anyone else could either."

Rex rubbed his chin. "Are you sure you're not covering for someone else?"

"I'm not. I deal with numbers, cold, hard facts. If one of the people I know killed Eloise, they'll have to face the consequences. I'll understand why they might have been driven to do it, but I can't condone violence."

Although it appeared they'd come to the end of the interview, Marla wasn't quite ready for it. "Tell us what you know about her ex-husband as well as Grace Adamson, Tanner Oliver or Chloe Reardon." She caught sight of Rex's brow raising briefly.

"I can give you a thumbnail description of each of them, but I just told you, I don't think any of them is capable of murder."

"It would help us get to know those individuals better," Rex said.

"Okay, but as you've probably already discovered, I'm not much of a people person. I don't read others well."

"Do your best," Rex said.

She released a long breath. "I guess I know Grace best. She's creative; that's the only reason Essy has done as well as it has. She's honest and hard-working. But business was not her strong suit. That's why Eloise was able to come in and grab such a strong hold of Essy to the point of buying out Grace four years ago. Although Grace got the money, selling her baby hurt her spirit. She hasn't been able to put something new together since. PR is what she knows, and she signed a two-year noncompete clause when she sold to Eloise."

This was the first they'd heard of the noncompete clause. It could be a strong motivation for murder.

"I don't know whether Tanner worshiped Eloise or is just ambitious. Whichever, he has been willing to do almost anything to please her, short of anything unethical."

"How do you know he wouldn't do anything unethical?" Rex asked.

"Because he'd sometimes complain to me about assignments she'd given him, not sure whether he could go through with them."

"Could you give us an example?" Marla asked.

"He confided in me. I don't feel comfortable giving you specifics. But occasionally she'd ask him to lie to a client. Usually those were white lies about her availability or some minor action. We talked about how he could meet her expectations and not outright lie. He also was concerned about Chloe's growing importance to Eloise. He thought she was playing Eloise. I tried to tell him Eloise wasn't the kind of person who could be played."

"Thank you for sharing that," Marla said. "It gives us a better picture of their relationship."

"I don't know Chloe that well. She has always been friendly to me but friendly in a patronizing way. You know, saying nice things you're not sure she means?"

Marla and Rex nodded as encouragement for her to continue.

"She seemed to just show up one day. After that, she was everywhere. Or so it seemed. Whenever Eloise had some minor question about the budget, she'd send Chloe to see me. If Eloise couldn't make it to a staff meeting, she'd have Chloe step in for her. Not as an equal, of course, but as her representative. Everything Chloe said appeared to be what Eloise had told her to say.

"I knew Brecken in the days when he and Eloise were married and I saw him at social gatherings. More recently, we've played on the pickleball team but not as partners. I don't know why he participated, because Eloise was always telling him what he'd done wrong."

She stopped and looked at them expectantly.

"Thank you. We appreciate your insights," Marla said. "Would you go back to Essy now that she's gone?" she asked as an afterthought.

"I don't know. I was only let go recently, so I haven't been looking. I've used this time away from the company to heal. Not from being fired but to get through my grief."

"Do you have any idea who will take over?" Rex asked. "As the accountant, you might've seen various documents or plans outlining what would happen in the event of the owner's death."

"At one time, while she was still married, she named her

husband to succeed her if anything were to happen to her. It was for a loan document, where she had to provide proof that Essy wouldn't suffer in the event of her death. She named him because he was the obvious party, but she joked about doing it. She never took the possibility of her death seriously."

"Why do you think that was?" Marla asked.

Nell took a moment to consider. "Good question. Somewhere along the way Eloise reinvented herself to someone who didn't need anyone else to do her bidding. She wasn't like that when she first joined the company. Maybe after she lost two babies she hardened her heart. I'm not a psychiatrist, so I can only speculate about what happened to her. Whatever it was, she didn't think about planning for the future, other than expanding the business sooner than it was probably ready."

"It would seem like someone who was so into herself like you've described Eloise would make a lot of enemies," Marla said.

"Enemies?" Nell replied. "More like victims. But that doesn't mean any of them killed her."

"Are you afraid of repercussions if you name someone?" Rex asked.

"Not at all. Like I've told you, I deal in numbers and facts. If something or someone seemed out of kilter to me, I'd say so."

There didn't seem to be much more to say at this point. Marla had run out of ways to challenge Nell's stance.

Rex gave Nell his card, and they left.

Marla was stumped. Was the woman trying to mislead them, or did she really believe none of her cohorts was guilty? She couldn't wait to process this interview with Rex.

thirteen

. . .

"**D**oes she really believe none of the people she described would kill her former boss?" Marla asked as soon as they were both inside the SUV, even before she buckled in. "I heard a possible motive in every one of her descriptions."

"Do you think that was intentional?"

"I didn't get that impression, but this was our first time meeting her," Marla said. She thought about that last statement. "It frustrates me that we can't get all the information we need from just one interview."

"Is that why you attempted to jump into it immediately with her when you went right to the argument on the court last Saturday?" he asked.

"I saw your reaction. It was brief, and I'm sure she didn't notice, but I knew you weren't happy with my question."

"Your question was fine. It just seemed a little premature. My style is to warm up a little first."

She laughed. "Really? Could've fooled me. You're Mr. Direct. No beating around the bush with you."

He didn't reply. Instead, he focused on his driving.

"Rex? I said that in a friendly way. It wasn't meant as an insult."

"Why don't you call Grace and tell her we're on our way."

She apparently had insulted him even though she hadn't meant to. Should she try to make things right or wait until later? Their arrival at Grace's house settled that question.

The former owner of Essy lived in a modest bungalow in a quiet neighborhood in West St. Paul. Only a couple of cars were parked on the street at this time of day. The yards were all well-kept. A few houses down, a dog barked at their arrival and strained to escape the fence keeping it safely away from them.

Everything seemed so ordinary. Who'd have thought they were here pursuing a murder investigation?

Grace came to the door immediately. "Come in. I've been expecting someone from the police department to show up." She stared at Marla, her hazel eyes curious. "You're Marla Dane! You were handing out water at pickleball last Saturday."

"Ms. Dane and I are consulting with the police on this case," Rex said. "Anything you would say to them, you can say to us. And vice versa."

"Mr. Alcorn and I worked with them before because we were familiar with many of the persons of interest in a case. So we were asked to help again with this case."

"Where can we talk?" Rex asked.

"Would you mind coming to the kitchen? I'll be more relaxed around the kitchen table."

They followed her through an archway that led immediately to the kitchen but waited for her to show them where to sit.

"Where do we start?" she asked before they had a chance to take the lead.

"How about telling us how you know the deceased and your relationship with her," Rex said.

Elbows on the table, she folded her hands and leaned into

them. "Tall order because there's so much. I guess I'll start at the beginning. I started the company eleven years ago with a small inheritance from my grandfather. I'd been out of college a few years and was making my way up the ladder in a large entertainment representation agency in New York City. In order to claim my inheritance, which was a considerable sum of money, I had to agree to relocate to the Twin Cities and remain at least five years. My grandmother had predeceased my grandfather by a few years, but they had both been disappointed when I left town. Other than coming back and staying for five years, I could do anything I wanted with the money.

"It wasn't easy leaving my career in New York, which had taken time to establish. At least I didn't have to say goodbye to someone close to me. I'd been engaged years before, but that didn't work out. There'd been no one since. I chose to start my own PR firm. That's what I'd planned to do in college until I got the job working with fledgling actors. I was so inexperienced in that field, I chose to call myself Springboard Concepts, instead of coming right out and using PR in the title. That was my first lesson in PR. I wanted to show potential clients how creative I was. I quickly learned that in order to get those clients in the first place, they had to find you. That didn't happen with an esoteric title, brilliant as I thought mine was. So I shortened it to its first initials, SC. And that name quickly morphed to Essy."

She stopped. "That was more than you wanted to know. I'll move ahead. Despite the name change, Essy grew slowly. I faced a lot of competition here in the Twin Cities area. Companies that had been around much longer, that were larger with established reputations. I only had one advantage: myself. I'm good at what I do. Not only am I creative, but my time in New York introduced me to an entertainment network not all my competitors enjoyed. But it was a constant struggle to stay on top of each client's needs and still expand the business. I needed an assistant. Enter Eloise."

"When was that?" Rex asked.

"About nine years ago. Eloise came to me on the recommendation of her husband, Brecken. I'd known him from school years before and ran into him by chance at a local nursery. They'd been unemployed for a few months, and though he didn't say so, he seemed rather desperate. He briefly described her qualifications, which meshed to a certain degree with what I was seeking. I didn't do any further recruiting. In retrospect, probably not a good idea.

"She came across as likable, agreeable and very interested in helping me do my job better. Those qualities soon began to fade, although she changed so seamlessly, it was months before I noticed. I was unveiling a client plan and noting the tasks I was assigning her and she simply said, 'That doesn't make any sense. I'll handle the initial presentation instead of you.' Up until then, she'd say things like, 'Why don't I do X instead?' or 'Here's another suggestion.' But that day she came right out and told me what she would do."

"How did you react to that?" Marla asked.

"I was so surprised, I went along with her. And wouldn't you know? She did great. I couldn't very well turn her down the next time she said she'd take the lead, and that's how she began to make herself indispensable. Six months later, she asked for a promotion, or should I say, demanded I recognize her efforts. Next, it was a bonus. She'd saved my bacon by remembering a project deadline I'd overlooked. It wasn't until after I'd sold the business to her that she bragged about intentionally misfiling my reminder notes.

"She'd only been there five years when I had no choice but make her partner. I wanted to expand the business and needed the money she was ready to invest. She seized upon my expansion plans and made them her own, all the time letting clients know who the real brains of the business was. Even with that track record, I wasn't prepared for her to take over more and more of the leadership and decision-making from me. She claimed she was sparing me from having to deal with the day-to-day details so I could focus my mind on the bigger picture, finding new clients. But every time I thought I had a fresh lead, I discovered she'd gotten there first."

"And then what happened?" Marla asked, giving the woman a chance to breathe.

"My old clients began making excuses why they couldn't meet with me. Eventually they outright told me they preferred the service they were receiving from Eloise. When I confronted her about what had been happening, she told me I was the one who was hurting the business and that if I didn't do something about it soon, we might even lose the business. When I foolishly asked her what exactly that meant, she came right out and told me to sell Essy to her. I laughed at first, but within a few weeks, as my first and favorite client told me she'd rather deal with Eloise, I agreed to discuss the sale. I was lucky Brecken was around to coach me how to negotiate a fair price, or I might have sold too low."

Her discourse had taken her inside her own thoughts, but now she appeared to realize how long she'd been going on. "That was much more than you asked for. Once I got started, I couldn't stop."

"But very helpful," Rex said. "I never met the victim, and Ms. Dane only met her briefly. You've helped us understand how it was that she took over your business."

"But it's still not clear to me how it happened without you realizing what was afoot," Marla said.

Grace nodded. "I get that. It still confounds me how I could be so blind. All I can say is that Eloise was a force like

I'd never known. She could be so ingratiating and yet so slippery."

"Where did she get the funding to buy into a partnership and later to purchase the company?" Marla asked.

"You haven't heard that part? About five and a half years ago, she won the lottery. She cleared about seven million. Of all people to benefit from one of those sweepstakes, leave it to Eloise. I did my due diligence. My financial advisors assured me she still had most of what she'd won."

"Did you involve your own accountant, Nell Hampton, in this transaction?"

"Nell and I went way back to almost the beginning of Essy. She intimately knew every detail of the company, and I trusted her judgment. I involved her from the beginning of my decision to sell. I hated having gotten myself in that position and turned to her for advice about how to get out of it. We spent many hours debating the pros and cons of several options, but in the end, neither of us could see my way out. I needed the continued confidence of my clients, and everywhere I turned, she seemed to have taken that away from me."

"Was the parting amicable?" Marla asked.

Grace sniffed. "What do you think? No, but I kept my cool as best I could. I learned long ago not to burn bridges."

"Why did you agree to be part of the pickleball team?" Rex asked. "The woman took your business away from you, the business you worked so hard to build."

"It hasn't been easy. Besides reminding me in her own subtle way how she'd beaten me at my own game, the PR business, and boasting about how much more successful it now was without me, she has been an unrelenting team captain, constantly telling me what I'd done wrong and how I was hurting the team. But I wanted to maintain contact with my former associates, Nell and

Tanner, to get updates on the so-called success she'd been claiming. I dragged my feet reinvesting the proceeds from the sale, hoping someday I could buy it back. Crazy, maybe. But I kept hearing rumors that things weren't that great."

"Rumors?" Marla said. "From whom?" Neither Tanner nor Nell had mentioned that the business was suffering. Would they have told the former owner it was?

"I guess it's okay to talk about it now that she's gone. Nell obviously is unhappy at being fired, but even before that, she'd complain from time to time about Eloise's financial decisions. And ever since Chloe came on the scene, Tanner has thought he was being replaced."

She seemed to stop short of saying more. This from the woman who'd gone on extensively about her relationship with the dead woman.

"Anyone else?" Marla asked, attempting to get Grace to finish out her thought.

"Uh, mostly those two. Occasionally Brecken would say something."

"Brecken?" Rex asked. "Where was he getting his information? He never worked there and was no longer married to the woman."

"You'd have to ask him that," Grace replied, backing away from her previous statement.

"Let's talk about last Saturday," Marla said. "We heard there was an argument on the court before play. What was your part in it?"

"I was an onlooker. Even though she was no longer part of Essy, Nell wanted to have it out with Eloise over a recent purchase. I think I heard it was an apartment, although it didn't make sense to me why Eloise would think she needed one. She has—had a beautiful home in St. Paul."

"You didn't get involved, express your opinion?"

"No, that was the last thing I wanted to do, get into it with Eloise. But I did want to learn more about why Nell was fired. Since the two of us are no longer with Essy, I thought maybe we could partner up on another project. It was just an idea at the time but enough to make me stay close on the sidelines."

"And afterwards? Were you able to make contact with Ms. Hampton?"

"No. She took off right after the match, and we haven't had a chance to talk since then. And now with Eloise's death, things are different."

Marla couldn't resist the opening. "Different? How?"

"Neither of us cared much for Eloise. But we never wanted or expected her life to end like it did. Being murdered. My brain hasn't really grasped the horror of it all. If Essy continues, who will lead it? One or both of us may have a chance to go back. But so much is still up in the air. Eloise's killer has to be found. And no one seems to know the terms of her will."

"Who do you suspect killed her?" Rex asked, returning to the key question.

"I didn't, if that's what you're asking. Nor do I think Nell or Brecken did. I can't say about Tanner or Chloe. And I don't know Liz that well."

"That said, is there anything else you can tell us that relates to the murder?" Marla asked.

Grace studied a fingernail a few beats.

"Ms. Adamson?" Marla prompted. "Is there something else you'd like to share?"

"I don't know if it's pertinent to your investigation, and I'd hate to get anyone in trouble needlessly."

"Let us judge how pertinent it is," Rex said.

"It's about Chloe Reardon. If you haven't looked into her

background, I hope you would consider doing so. I still don't understand why Eloise hired her."

"Thank you. Can you share an example of your thinking?"

Grace took a moment to consider. "I was gone by the time she was hired, but both Tanner and Nell were surprised and skeptical when she first came on board. There'd been no formal recruitment or hiring process, although I guess she'd already worked for Eloise as an intern. When Nell told Eloise there was no budget for new staff, she was told to rearrange proposed expenditures and make it happen."

Marla wasn't tracking. Why would Chloe's background or how she was hired make her a killer? "Aside from how she was hired, do you have any other concerns about Chloe Reardon?" she asked.

"Everything I've heard about her from Nell and Tanner suggests unbridled ambition that would hesitate at nothing to get ahead. As the one who's been betrayed by Eloise in the past, I'd say she deserved whatever she got from Chloe. Anything short of murder."

"Thanks," Rex told her. He offered her his card and asked her to get in touch if anything else occurred to her.

They left right after that.

Rex shook his head as they drove off. "What did you think about Grace's suggestion we look deeper into Chloe's background?"

"I'm not sure. It could be she was trying to deflect our investigation off herself and her friends by steering us toward Chloe. Or as a third party, she may have heard things about Chloe from her friends that concerned her. She struck me as pretty level-headed, even though Eloise Wallace managed to steal her company from her."

"She didn't have to warn me about Chloe," Rex replied.

"After you left last night, I checked out that flick you mentioned yesterday. *All About Eve*? I found an article describing how the film depicts the classic trope of the younger actress seeking to replace the older actress. We definitely have to give her a closer look."

fourteen

. . .

Marla was about to call Chief Goodhue to update him on their morning when he called her instead. "I took a chance that you'd be finished interviewing the last two people on your list. It's a little early, but can you and Rex meet me for lunch in fifteen minutes? I'd like to get an in-person update, plus I'll have my own updates for you."

They agreed to meet at a Chinese restaurant a couple of blocks from the condo complex. Goodhue was already there at a back table when they arrived.

"First, tell me about your morning," he said.

Rex gave a quick rundown on Nell. "Attempted to be open and cooperative, but she's still grieving her late wife as well as smarting from being fired by the victim a few weeks ago."

"What's your gut telling you about her as a suspect?" Goodhue asked.

"Guess it's possible. She took her role as accountant seriously and was incensed by Eloise Wallace's supposed misuse of company funds. But if pushed too far, I see her as calling out her former boss to the authorities rather than killing her."

"And your second interview?" Goodhue asked.

"Grace Adamson," Marla said. "She maybe had the strongest motive to kill Eloise. The woman essentially stole her company from her. Given that history, I still don't understand why she's continued to play on the pickleball team. She said it was because she wanted to stay in touch with Tanner Oliver and Nell Hampton in case there was a chance she could get Essy back."

Goodhue leaned forward and placed his folded handed on the tabletop. "In other words, you haven't eliminated anyone yet." Disappointment underlay his tone.

"There's no clear-cut suspect, Goodhue," Rex replied. "The woman stepped on many toes. We don't want to leap to any conclusion too soon."

"I appreciate that you've had a lot of information to sift through in a short amount of time. You've done a great job establishing the basics. Continue to chop away at it. Just, uh ..."

"Get it solved as fast as we can," Rex finished for him. "Though we're not even close."

Marla couldn't believe Rex would admit as much to the chief. Even with Rex now consulting for his former competitor, his relationship with Goodhue didn't appear to have been repaired. At least not completely. "What Rex meant is that there's more underlying the ties all six people we've interviewed had to Eloise, which we still need to discover. I sense there's one key piece of information just waiting to be found, and when we do, it will be the key to finding our killer."

She didn't dare check out Rex's expression. He probably didn't appreciate her attempting to clarify his statement.

"That's very optimistic, Marla," Goodhue replied. "Rex and I both know murder cases sometimes take a long time before resolution. Some never get solved. Convincing the public and the media of that is another thing."

"Marla's got a point," Rex said, surprising her with his support. "We've got our hands full with this case because there were so many people close to her who hated her. We need to keep going over their statements with them, waiting for one or more of them to slip up. That's gonna happen, hopefully sooner rather than later. Marla and I are finding our stride working together. She follows up when I don't see connections and vice versa."

That was unexpected. Did he not want to cave so soon with Goodhue or did he really mean it? She'd love to ask him that question when it was just the two of them, but she was also learning he'd reveal more in his own time rather than her pressing him.

Goodhue addressed her. "Is that true, Marla? Investigating homicides is replacing your love of acting?"

Oh, boy! She wasn't expecting that question. "Truthfully, Chief, I have no idea how to reply. Figuring out my own life right now seems even more complicated than this case. But you've given me something to hold on to while I repair that part of my life."

"I appreciate the honesty," Goodhue replied. "I kinda hope you'll keep doing what you are now, even after you two put this case to bed. Whether it was all the indirect training you received playing a PI or you've just quickly picked up investigation techniques, you're showing a real knack for it. We've been lucky to have your help."

Rex didn't say anything, but he didn't counter Goodhue's words, either.

"That said, let's move on to my other news," Goodhue said. "The autopsy and tox reports are in. Our initial assessment was confirmed. It was arsenic poisoning. There were still traces of it in her water bottles as well as her blood. She died between midnight Saturday night and midnight Sunday. Whoever poisoned her had a rudimentary understanding of how the stuff works. Gave her a dose that didn't take effect immediately but was strong enough to kill her within twenty-four hours. I'll send you the details."

"Arsenic, huh?" Rex said. "I thought the stuff had been pretty much outlawed in most over-the-counter products. Although I guess it could be found in older products. Or labs that don't mind looking the other way."

Marla weighed in. "It was the culprit at least once a season on *Carruthers*. The writers liked it because it was clear and taste-less and supposedly easy to administer."

"We still need to determine when she came in contact with it."

"She appeared to be fine at the pickleball match Saturday morning but may have been starting to feel the effects Saturday night. Her assistant, Chloe Reardon, texted her. Eloise replied, but according to Chloe, her response was more abbreviated than usual."

"Good to know, which means we can proceed on the assumption she was most likely poisoned at the match. The one officer I could spare canvassed the neighborhood and deter-mined no one saw her leave or witnessed anyone arriving during the Saturday through Sunday period. The text to Chloe Reardon that you mentioned was the last activity on her phone. Her secu-rity system wasn't engaged overnight."

"It would appear she died alone," Marla said. "How ironic for someone who was so self-involved."

Marla's words halted further discussion for several beats.

"I've got other information to share with you," Goodhue said at length, "the background research on the victim and the six potential suspects minus financial data. Had to obtain warrants on those details, so they're taking longer. My intern did a remarkable job gathering and putting together these profiles in just a day."

"Good! We'll combine our debriefing of this morning's interviews with a review of your intern's best efforts," Rex said.

"Then I'll let you get on with it," Goodhue said, rising. "Keep me posted. Enjoy your meal."

"Are you okay with eating here, now that Goodhue has said his piece?" Rex asked once it was just the two of them.

"How about we get our meal to go? I'm anxious to go somewhere private to discuss the reports Goodhue sent us," she said.

"Sounds like a plan," he returned.

They didn't say much during the short trip back to the condo building. Each seemed to be thinking their own thoughts. Marla returned to Kitty's condo first because she hadn't seen her sister since the day before.

"There you are," Kitty said, as if Marla had been gone for weeks.

Marla followed Kitty into the kitchen. "I stopped by to see how your pie presentation went last night."

Kitty clapped her hands together, pleased with herself. "He literally ate it up," she replied, chuckling at her own pun. "He ate two pieces then and begged me to leave the rest with him when he brought me home. We were a success!"

"We. At least you give Rex and me credit for our part."

"Uh ... if Hub ever comments about it to you, please keep the part you two played in the project to yourself."

"Will that ever happen? Neither Rex nor I have yet to meet him." And if his stint as Kitty's latest beau, or whatever they were called these days, continued along the same timeline as the rest of her romantic interests, Marla doubted they ever would.

"I need to get past a small issue that Hub had with the pie first," Kitty said in sweet, coaxing tone.

Small issue? "I thought you said he really liked it," Marla said, waiting for the bomb to drop.

"We overlooked a critical point."

"I know I shouldn't ask, but what was that?" Marla asked.

"The type of flour we used. Even though Hub praised what we made, his first question was whether I used his product. It would have been so easy to say yes, but for some reason, probably your influence, I told him the truth. I'd just started seeing Hub when you and I went grocery shopping, and it never occurred to me that sometime down the road the type of flour we used would become critical. Besides, it's higher priced than the one we picked."

"Good for you. It would've been so easy to have told him what he wanted to hear."

Kitty smiled expectantly. "Thanks, but he didn't drop it there. He wants another pie. This one using Prairie Harvest Flour. He even offered to bring me a complimentary bag."

This pie thing was taking on a life of its own. "Hold on. You want Rex and me to help you make another pie? That won't be possible right now. Our investigation of Eloise Wallace's murder is heating up. We need to focus on it." If she'd ever wanted to meet this new man in her sister's life, she wasn't so sure now. What a demanding jerk!

Kitty's smile continued. "I wasn't asking the two of you to do a repeat performance. Hub wants to sit in and watch me make it myself. Tomorrow night."

Make that demanding *super* jerk. "He doesn't trust you to actually use his company's flour?"

Kitty rubbed her neck. "I suppose that could be his intent, but it's more likely he's got some idea in mind for another way to promote his product."

"Something that includes you?"

"Omigosh, I hadn't considered that possibility," Kitty replied. "I've been more focused on having to prove my baking skills to him."

Marla voiced her thoughts out loud. "My sister, the star of flour commercials. Interesting turn of events. You before the camera instead of me."

"Hold on, besides it not being a done deal, he hasn't even broached the idea yet," Kitty said. She tilted her head, apparently picturing herself pitching Prairie Harvest Flour.

"Would you consider it if asked?"

"And you accuse me of leaping to conclusions. I don't know. Maybe. No, it will never happen once he sees me in action in the kitchen."

Marla was about to reassure Kitty that she and Rex would help her look good for this new guy when it hit her. Her sister had tried to set her up. "That 'poor me' act won't work with me, sister dear. If you wanted Rex and me to walk you through how to do this, why didn't you just ask?"

Kitty puckered her lips. "Can't fool you, can I? You and Rex have so much on your plate right now, I was afraid to come right out and ask for another favor. But I like this guy. I don't want to lose him over this silly pie thing."

Marla relaxed her shoulders. "At least you came clean now. Look, Rex and I will need to take a dinner break later on. I'll see if he'll agree to eat here while we give you a quick lesson."

Kitty hugged her. "Thank you, thank you, thank you. Tell me what you want to eat, and I'll order out while we talk."

"I can't speak for Rex. He may feel his helpfulness has run its course."

"But you'll still be here, right?"

"Unless something else pops up with the case, yes. But Kitty, even if you can pull off this demo for Hub, you need to tell him you're not a baker or your relationship is in trouble."

"I know. I just like this guy so much, I got carried away trying to impress him."

"I'll text you when Rex and I decide to take a break. We'll take you up on that offer for dinner." She pivoted at the door as a new thought hit. "And it won't be cheap."

fifteen

. . .

"You do not have to help Kitty yet another time," Marla told Rex ten minutes later, after joining him at his condo and briefing him on Kitty's latest request.

"I've never known your sister to be quite so pushy. Are you a bad influence on her?" he joked.

"It's not me. It's this Hub Sherman. She's so taken with him, she'll do about anything, within reason I hope, to keep him interested in her."

"How long do we have to examine all the information we've obtained today before we have to break for this lesson?"

"It's about twelve forty now. If we break at six, we'll have at least five hours to determine if we've found a new lead," she replied.

Rex stared at her, one brow raised. "How did you do that?"

"What?"

"You didn't look at your watch or the clock in the room," he said.

"Oh, that. It's just something I can do, know what time it is, or at least something reasonably close."

"Is it a trait you inherited?"

"Not that I'm aware. But then, I don't have Kitty's perfect pitch, either."

"The woman who doesn't know how to bake a pie has perfect pitch?" he said.

"Ask her to start a song sometime."

Rex chuckled. "This talent for knowing the time? Did it come in handy when you were acting?"

"Just the opposite. I knew exactly how late shooting was going whenever the director took us into overtime. I would've preferred being kept in the dark then. Just believing we were running a little late rather than exactly how late."

"I'll look to you from now on to keep us on schedule," he said. "I just wish I possessed some special quality I could contribute to our efforts."

"Are you fishing for a compliment?"

"No, not at all. I'd like to contribute my own special talent to this partnership."

"Excuse me? Rex Alcorn finds himself lacking in one tiny area?"

"Don't kid me, Marla. I was being sincere."

"Oh. It's just that you're always so sure of yourself. It's difficult to picture you as anything else."

"Boy, have I put one over on you," he said, wonderingly.

"C'mon, Rex. Ever since the day you helped me bring my baggage in out of the rain, you've made it your purpose to let me know the awe I should show to be in your presence."

"Are you deliberately trying to start a fight?"

"No! Of course not. Maybe we should get on to the matter at hand?"

"You don't want to get into whatever it is I've done that has put you off? I was under the impression the two of us had resolved our initial differences and were now getting on quite well? But if you'd prefer to spar ...?"

"No, I'd rather not. Never mind what I've been saying. You're right. We have been getting along ever since somewhere in the middle of the Elliot case. Far be it from me to mess that up now."

"I did a quick review of the personal profiles Goodhue sent us while Kitty was playing on your sisterly concern. Too bad we didn't have the profile on Eloise available before we began our interviews. We might've structured our questions differently."

"Give me a minute to do my own quick read-through," she said.

Eloise grew up in Blue Earth, Minnesota. There were few notes on her early years other than her dad was an occasional farm worker who supplemented his income driving trucks cross-country. Her mother was a secretary at the local high school. She was a C+ student in high school but managed to get into the University of Minnesota with a high ACT score. In high school she was involved in one school activity, the flag corps ladies who performed at school athletic activities.

She dropped out of college the middle of her junior year because her grades were suffering. That same year she took a business course. After that, she temped as an office worker/clerk for the next year until she was hired by a hardware store on a full-time basis. She worked there for seven years until the owner retired. Her next employer was DeGrassi Manufacturing, where she met Brecken Wallace and worked her way up through the clerical support ranks. After a short honeymoon in Chicago, they moved into an apartment in the older part of St. Paul and lived there a year and a half before buying an older bungalow in West St. Paul. Eighteen months later, they were out of jobs. After her fifteen years at DeGrassi, Eloise went back to temping while she apparently looked for other full-time work.

They were more familiar with the rest. Grace Adamson hired her as an executive assistant three months after their layoff, and five years later, Eloise became her partner. A year later—four years ago —she bought out Grace and ran the business alone from there on.

The only information listed after that was a series of photos showing her with various clients.

"Not much new stuff here, other than more on her early years," Rex said after she finished reading the profile. "Our suspects have been on track there. Anything strike you as unusual?"

"Although there are a lot of stories of business leaders who succeeded despite their poor educational beginnings, it still seems odd to me that someone who barely got into college except for her ACT score and then dropped out of college could go on to run her own PR firm."

"I suppose," Rex replied, "but don't forget that ACT score you mentioned. The woman possessed native intelligence. That, coupled with ambition and ruthlessness, can take someone far."

"Her ex said her personality changed after her miscarriages, but there's nothing about them in the profile."

"Medical records are private," he reminded her. "We can probably find hospital and doctor bills once we get her financials."

Rex poured them glasses of water. "Drinking this stuff always seems to clear my head when there's a lot of details to absorb."

Funny. It didn't strike him odd that they'd be clearing their heads with purportedly the same liquid that had killed the woman whose case they were investigating. She left that thought unsaid. "Are we ready to move on to the other profiles?"

"Yeah, I've got enough Eloise Wallace in my head for now," he said.

"Should we debrief on our interviews this morning or move

right into the other profiles?" she asked. "Or are you content with what we told Goodhue?"

"I only gave Goodhue enough information to satisfy him for the moment. I picked up a lot more from our meeting with Nell," he said.

"Okay. Tell me."

"From the hints she dropped about Eloise's financial dealings, an immediate audit would seem to be in order."

"I'm not all that familiar with business matters. Until recently, I left most of my money dealings to my financial managers. But won't that be a matter of course before anyone is allowed to assume leadership of Essy?" she asked.

"You'd think. But with no succession plan in place, it's hard to say what will happen next as far as Essy is concerned. That was my overriding takeaway from the interview. How about you?"

"I was more impressed with the woman's emotional state. She is still grieving the loss of her wife. She doesn't look well, and her thrown-together state of dress suggests she's paying no attention to her grooming. She never should've gone back to work so soon. She said something about her head not being in it, which would explain the work problems we heard about. And Eloise was unsympathetic enough to Nell's situation to fire her for performance issues. That could be a very strong motive for murder, except that the woman we saw didn't seem emotionally up to it."

"She said she was let go because she challenged the purchase of the apartment," Rex said.

"Which may or may not have been reason enough to let her go, or Eloise could've been planning to do so for some time. Nell hadn't been afraid to confront her like Tanner and Chloe were."

"Do you want to go over her background report now that we've set the stage?" he asked.

"Let's try that approach."

They pulled the report on Nell up on their respective phones. It covered what they already knew about the woman. That her background was in accounting, that she'd been with Essy for ten years and that she'd been married to Katharine Miles until her recent death. It also said she'd grown up in the area, gave her age as thirty-seven, and said she had one sister who lived in Hastings, Minnesota, and a brother who lived in Chicago. What was a bit of a shock was that her minor in college was chemistry. She might know something about arsenic.

Marla finished reading. "We got most of what we needed to know about her from her directly," she said, "other than her personal background and financial situation."

"And don't forget the minor in chemistry," Rex added.

"There was that. She's got enough of a nest egg that she'll be able to survive without having to get a new job for a while, so payback for the loss of her job wouldn't have been a strong motive, except for her emotional state. Couple that with her knowledge of chemistry, which could include poisons, and she's right back at the top of our list."

"That was my take as well," Rex said. "Although it's been well over a decade since she finished college. Even if she did learn about poisons then, she could've forgotten all that unless she's taken a course or done some research recently."

"Can Goodhue or his sources get hold of her recent Internet searches or checkouts from the library?"

"I get what you're thinking and yes, it's possible, although he'd probably have to get a warrant to check out either. Most likely he'd want to be assured we're closer to naming her Suspect Number One before taking that step."

"Okay, I get it. Maybe we'll be closer to that point once we've gone through the rest of these reports," she said. "Let's move on to Grace. Like Nell, she was also harmed by Eloise Wallace."

"Harmed is a mild way of describing being knifed in the back by someone she brought on board to help her."

His statement caught her off guard. Her mind returned to her own situation in LA.

"Marla? You look miles away. What are you thinking about?"

"You said 'knifed in the back,' and that took me back to being replaced on *Carruthers*. The network, ever conscious of the changing demographics of our audience, pushed our showrunner to bring in younger talent. Personally, I think he could've stood his ground with them and resisted their so-called ultimatum, but he's ambitious and wants to climb even higher in the Hollywood hierarchy, so he caved. He didn't exactly knife me in the back, but it felt like that at the time. I wasn't expecting it."

"Do you think Grace was on to Eloise's plans to take over Essy?" Rex asked, returning to the subject at hand. "Or do you think she actually was knifed in the back?"

"She told us she couldn't believe she hadn't seen it coming."

"But she also said Eloise was a force like she'd never known. To me, that says the victim was a master of pulling the wool over Grace's eyes."

"One can feel mighty foolish when they remove the wool. Enough to want revenge?" she asked.

"Have you ever felt like that given what happened to you?"

Interesting question. Until she'd put her life as an actress on hold and come to Minnesota, did she ever want to retaliate against the powers that be?

"Marla? Did I go too far bringing up your situation? I thought we'd gotten to a point where it was safe for me to mention your former life."

"You're fine, Rex. I only paused because I was trying to think back to my feelings since it all happened. Truthfully, yes, there've been times when I wanted retribution against those who dismissed me or didn't fight for me or support me. But I never followed through. And the thought of killing anyone never occurred to me."

He reached across the table where they sat and took her hand. "Thanks. Good to know I haven't read our relationship wrong."

"I've told you things I haven't shared with anyone else. Even Kitty. You seemed to know I couldn't bottle up my feelings forever. I needed to vent."

"Thanks. Good to know I didn't misjudge things."

Regretfully, she released his hand. She wasn't ready to think about what might be happening between them. Not yet. "But we've only started to explore my feelings. And to go further would mean you sharing more of yourself, too. I don't think you're ready for that. Or ever will be," she told him.

Even though he was no longer holding her hand, he didn't back away. "You're a wise woman, Marla Dane. I'm not ready." He paused as if debating whether to say more. "But never say never."

sixteen

. . .

Grace Adamson might have gone on at length about the history of Essy, but her report contained even more information about her background, particularly the years before she started the company. She was born in St. Paul and grew up in a modest household in Roseville. Her father was a professor of American history at the University of Minnesota, and her mother was a large-animal vet. She was an only child. Her paternal grandparents lived in Philadelphia, where her father had grown up. Her maternal grandparents owned a pharmacy in downtown St. Paul. In her youth, they expanded to Minneapolis, Duluth, Rochester, Winona and St. Cloud. By the time she graduated from high school, they had assembled a minor empire and had become quite wealthy.

For reasons the report did not cover, she attended college in New York City and stayed on there to work at a small entertainment management agency. Her parents were killed in an automobile accident while she was in college. Her paternal grandfather died while she was in high school. The paternal grandmother passed away during Grace's third year post-college. As she had told them, her maternal grandfather died when she was in her early thirties. The report cited the contents of his will, which had been probated a year later. Essy, or at that time Springboard Concepts, was established a year later. There was little noted about Essy until she partnered with Eloise five years ago and then the sale a year later.

There were no other personal details about her. She had never been married. Nor had the intern found details about any romantic liaisons she might have had over the years, male or female.

"What does this report tell you?" Marla asked Rex.

"Not much that we didn't already know, other than the details about the parents and grandparents. The fact that she's never been married or otherwise linked romantically is curious, don't you think?"

"You mean because she's a striking woman? It's okay. I agree, and like you, I'm surprised there has been no man in her life. Or any special someone."

"A question for us to ask her in our second interview." He checked his watch. "We're making good progress. What time is it?"

"One fifteen. Wait. Are you testing me?"

He made a face. "You caught that, huh? Sorry. Former cop instinct to verify a suspect's statement."

His action tickled her. Her time-telling trait had become so second nature to her that she'd forgotten how someone else might view it. But the last thing he said was too rich to ignore. "Suspect?" She let her voice rise. "I thought I'd been cleared as a person of interest in this case."

His hands came up surrender-style. "I was kidding, Marla. I thought you'd realize that."

She smiled. "I did, but it was too good an opening not to put you on the spot."

He blew out a breath. "Okay, I get it. I probably would've

done the same with you. But don't do it again. I don't take a joke as well as you."

Big admission. She was already on to that trait. She wouldn't tease him further. At least for a while. "Okay. Break over. Who's next?"

"I suppose we could tackle them in the same order we interviewed them, but I'm very curious about Chloe. Her rapid rise to prominence at Essy has me puzzled."

"Then Chloe it is," she replied.

Chloe had been raised by a single mother. There was little information about her father, including who he was. She was an only child. Her mother died from a severe case of influenza Chloe's first year of college when she was eighteen. It was later thought to have been an early case of COVID. No grandparents or other relatives were listed.

Her high school yearbook showed her participating in two plays and winning recognition as the lead in *Oklahoma*. She was also named as one of the school's emerging leaders for her work on the student council and as an after-school tutor.

She grew up in Minneapolis and graduated from the U of Minnesota with a degree in human resource development. As part of her degree requirements, she interned for Essy her senior year. It didn't say how or why she was assigned there versus another organization.

No other employment was listed.

"That's disappointing," Rex said after he finished reading it. "I hoped there'd be more. This doesn't tell us much more than we already knew."

Marla took a glance at what she'd just read. "The fact that she interned for Essy while she was still in college might explain why there was no recruiting. They already knew her and her work."

"I saw that, but it didn't ring any bells for me."

"One more thing. She was big into theater in high school. The acting part. Even though that was a few years back, it suggests a talent for playing a part. And her degree in human resource development tells us reading other people is a likely skill she picked up or enhanced."

"Good points," he replied. "But if acting is her thing, how will we ever get to the real Chloe Reardon?"

"I'd like to believe as an actress myself I'd be able to tell when she's playing a part and cut through it," she said.

"Clue me in when you pick up on those vibes so I can back you up however you choose to respond."

"I'm glad you said that, because the only way of cutting through her act that occurs to me is to respond to her in a way she's not anticipating. Something far-fetched."

"What do you have in mind?" he asked.

"Nothing right now. It'll have to be an inspiration of the moment. Improvised."

He narrowed his eyes like she was speaking in tongues.

"What? I'll try to give you a high sign to let you know what I'm doing, if that's what concerns you."

"Good to know, but do you hear yourself? When we first began this partnership, you were the one who questioned whether you could work without a script. To our benefit, that's worked out pretty well. But what you're proposing is on a different level. Will you be up to it?"

"I should be. That's a constant challenge in stage roles, when the other person forgets their lines or jumps ahead in the script, so it's not something totally outside my wheelhouse."

"All I can say is go for it, if the time is right."

"Are we done with Chloe? Who's next?"

"The ex-husband," Rex replied. "My gut tells me he's hiding his real feelings about his ex-wife. Correct that. He did tell us he didn't like her, but he didn't reveal the depth of those feelings. Let's see what more the intern has discovered."

Though a couple years older than Grace, Brecken had also grown up in Roseville and gone to the same high school. His high school yearbook showed a picture of them participating in chorus at the same time. An older brother, Preston, who now lived in Oak Park, Illinois, was married with three children. Their parents both worked for the University of Minnesota in support jobs. His father had been the head of maintenance until his retirement, and his mother had been a secretary in the dean's office. Brecken appeared to have taken advantage of the free tuition, having earned thirty-six credit hours due to his parents working for the institution, but he didn't finish.

He dropped out of school sometime during his sophomore year for unknown reasons. He seemed to disappear from the landscape for over ten years. He paid no taxes during that time.

Tax records started showing up about fifteen years ago when he started to work in facilities management for DeGrassi Manufacturing, where he met Eloise Carlson. They married thirteen years ago. They moved to St. Paul at the same time. Three years later, DeGrassi relocated its main plant to New Mexico and both the Wallaces were laid off. While he sought another position, Brecken took on odd jobs, including mowing lawns with a co-worker, Craig Jones, who had also lost his job. Six months later, they formed Wallace-Jones Lawn Care. The business remained small, just the two of them, for several years, although their tax returns indicated they'd seen steady growth in income.

The Wallaces were divorced six years ago.

Jones sold him his share of the business two years ago.

"Most of this tracks with what he told us, although there was little about Eloise," Marla said.

Next up was Liz. Though they now resided in the same building, Marla hadn't run into her except at the book club luncheon and at the match on Saturday, so reading her profile was a revelation. A local girl, she'd attended the school of fashion design affiliated with the U of Minnesota but had not graduated. Her employment record was spotty until a few years later, when she took a job as a nanny to a family in Connecticut. Following three years at that, she worked as a nighttime residence hall supervisor at a private girls' school, also in Connecticut, then signed on as buyer with a major women's clothing company headquartered in Massachusetts. That stint lasted nine years, until that business was acquired by a Dutch conglomerate and her division was eliminated.

However, it appeared she had survived that upheaval when they moved her to their executive staff in Amsterdam. Her stay there lasted almost five years. During that time she must have met and married an American entrepreneur, Wade Jenkins, because she/they relocated back to Atlanta, Georgia, in the States. There was no work history for the next several years, although the intern had located several media listings showing her and her husband at various social events.

Jenkins passed away twelve years ago. Liz remained in Georgia another year and then returned to the Twin Cities, where she bought the condo at Rambling Meadows. Since then, she'd become an investment consultant.

"I never would've guessed Liz has such a varied background," Marla said. "Although looking back, she's the one who's shown interest in Letitia's wardrobe."

"Interesting how she wound up back here after living on the East Coast, Georgia and even the Netherlands," Rex said.

"Kind of like the homing instinct with birds. No matter how far and wide they fly, most seem to find their way back to the roots of their origin."

He offered a collegial smile. "You mean like Marla Dane returning to Minnesota?"

"Yes and no. I did feel the need to 'come home' as the result of my problems in LA, but I'm not here permanently. Just to touch base."

He angled his head, all the while gazing directly at her. "Really? You've made up your mind about your next steps?" he asked, his tone failing to disguise a slight tinge of disappointment.

"Well, no. But coming back to Minnesota has always been a short-term solution for stepping away from my acting issues. Kitty's open invitation to stay with her has made it easy for me to do that."

"I thought you were enjoying being a real detective instead of playing one?"

"I am. But let's face it, homicides are a rarity around here, the two we've been following notwithstanding."

"Let's hope so," he replied. "But there shouldn't have to be a murder to keep you here."

"Why, Rex," she said, adopting a coquettish attitude, "is this your way of telling me you like having me around?"

He sat back and crossed his arms in front of him. "Me? I was talking about you. Your outlook seems to have changed ever since you arrived. You look healthier ... and happier."

Did she? Sometimes it took an outsider to see things one couldn't see for herself. "If that's what you're seeing, it's not at the expense of two dead people. It's just that I feel more involved here. More appreciated."

"That's important," he said. "Now I would *appreciate* it if you continued to share your reaction to her profile with me."

"Clever segue. The fashion thing was a bit of a surprise. The idea of creating her own line of evening wear for women seemed to come out of the blue when she told us, but now I can see that fashion has been a part of her background since college. I'd be interested in learning why she didn't finish the program and then why she took other unrelated jobs, like being a nanny and working in a girls' private school."

"Did you know she was a widow?" he asked.

"No. Kitty has never mentioned it. Maybe she doesn't know."

"I'm anxious to get the financials on all six of our interviewees plus on Eloise as well. In Liz's case, how much was in the estate of her late husband? It must've been enough to pay for her condo, but was there any left, since she's now working as an investment consultant?"

"Also, what was her connection to Eloise?" Marla asked. "She said she knew her from 'way back,' but what does that mean? When would they have known each other? Liz moved out of state right after she dropped out of fashion design school."

"A good question for Liz," he said.

"That leaves Tanner. What do we have on him?"

There wasn't much in his profile. He'd grown up in Mankato and come to the Twin Cities after graduating from St. Olaf with a degree in business administration. His first job had been with a national discount store. He left there after six months for an office job at a local nursery. He was there a year before being hired by Eloise as her assistant. That was right after she'd become the sole owner.

He lived three blocks from the Essy office in an apartment with two other roommates. He didn't appear to have any outside interests.

Rex set down his phone. "We've read through all six suspect profiles plus one for the victim. Where does that leave us?"

The answer that came to mind wasn't what they'd hoped for. "We still haven't eliminated anyone," she said.

seventeen

. . .

"Aren't you the optimistic one?" Rex said. He tipped up her chin with his index finger. "Don't look so forlorn. We've just begun to dig and actually unearthed quite a bit."

"What's your experienced cop's brain telling you?" she asked. "What exactly have we unearthed?"

"First, any one of at least five of the people we talked to had cause to kill Eloise. Even the sixth, Liz, could have, depending on how she knew the woman in the past. But cause doesn't mean action. It's still possible that they were all in it together, or two of them could've partnered up to take her out, but more than likely, only one of them did it. Which on the face of it, may sound near impossible, but in the end will get us our murderer, because the path will lead only to that one."

"I don't disagree, but you could've told me that two days ago before we got started."

"That was just Point One. We also know she was killed with poison, arsenic, to be exact."

"Which was established by the medical examiner, not us," she pointed out.

He stopped. "Be patient, Marla. I'm getting to that. Third,

none of them wanted to be on the pickleball team, but they all stayed and put up with her rants and demands week after week. What was it about last Saturday that set her death in motion?"

She perked up with that. "Maybe it wasn't just last Saturday, but that's when things, whatever they were, seemed to come to a head. Pickleball may have had nothing to do with her murder other than serving as the springboard."

"Clever."

"It was out before I realized the pun," she said. "Where does that leave us tonight?"

"Unless the financial information comes in, I'd say we rest our brains. Let's take Kitty up on that offer of a free dinner in exchange for the apple pie demonstration."

"Some free dinner, but I'm game," she replied.

She texted her sister with their order, beef burritos and refried beans—her stomach would pay afterwards—and the two of them left for Kitty's. They set up the equipment and ingredients while they waited for dinner.

"Your dinner should arrive in twenty minutes," Kitty told them. "You could've asked for a gourmet meal and I would've been happy to pay." She seated herself at one of the two stools around the kitchen island.

"What are you doing?" Marla asked her.

"Uh ...?"

"You're the performer tonight. It's our turn to sit here and observe," Marla said, exchanging a knowing look with Rex.

"Oh, right. Where do I start?"

"You have to ask?" Rex said. He shook his head. "Not a good sign, Kitty. If you're to pull this off, you have to convince this guy you're on top of things."

She nodded. "You're right." She rose and toddled around the island. She put a hand to her forehead like a mentalist guessing the contents of someone else's purse. She snapped out of her reverie in a few seconds. "Okay, let's get baking. First step, my apron." She pulled out a kitchen drawer and removed a bright pink chef's apron and slipped it on.

"That looks new," Marla said.

Kitty ran her hands down the front and beamed back at them. "It is! Do you like it? I bought it today. I needed something to inspire me."

It figured. But if a new apron would get her in the mood, so be it.

"Now that the costume is in place, what's next?" Rex asked.

"I guess I need to set up two staging areas, one for the crust and one for putting together the filling, sort of like the other night."

Marla nodded. Rex waited for the next steps, expressionless.

Kitty started slowly, then moved more quickly as her memory from the prior baking lesson returned. Three minutes later, she was set up. "Now what?" she asked.

"You tell us," Rex said.

"Uh, okay." She pressed her lips together. She carefully measured the flour into a large mixing bowl. She'd thought to place the bag of Prairie Harvest Flour in the spot of honor on the island counter.

Thus far, she hadn't said anything, intent on repeating exactly what she'd seen Rex and Marla do in their demo.

"Talk to us, Kitty," Marla said. "Tell us, or rather Hub, what you're doing at each step and why."

Kitty quickly doused the pained look on her face with a hopeful smile.

"Now I'm going to cut up the butter and flour it."

She was about to describe Rex's approach when her phone rang. "Can you grab that for me, Marla? My hands are all floury."

Marla picked up Kitty's phone.

"Hi, Kitty. It's Hub. I know I'm supposed to get my next pie tomorrow night, but I thought I'd surprise you and drop by tonight with that flour I promised you."

"Uh, hi, Hub. This is Marla, Kitty's sister. She's unable to come to the phone right now. Let me tell her you're here." She muted the phone. "He thought he'd surprise you by dropping by tonight."

"Omigod!" Kitty went even whiter than the flour covering her hands when she heard Marla talking to Hub.

"What should I tell him?" Marla asked.

"Send him away! He can't see me like this."

"He's already here, and he knows you're here, too. Time to bite the bullet, sis."

Kitty shot her an accusing look. "Did you set this up?"

"No, although I wish I'd thought of it. If you want to know him better, he needs to be introduced to all the crazy, wonderful facets of Kitty Lovejoy." Marla unmuted the phone. "Kitty says to come on up. You can help her finish the pie."

"You've got about a minute before he knocks on your door," Rex said, entering the sister-to-sister standoff. "How do you want to handle this?"

Kitty sent her a panicked expression. "What'll I do?"

"There's no time to clean all this up," Marla replied. "I'd say run with it."

"But I haven't even finished this first pie."

"He doesn't know that," Rex said. "Play it up."

Marla scuttled around the island, grabbed a fistful of flour and dabbed some of it on Kitty's face and the rest on her beautiful new apron.

"What are you doing?" Kitty screamed, attempting to wipe away the results of Marla's efforts.

"Forget about making him think pie making is a cinch for

you," Marla said, reapplying the white stuff. "Let him know it's not easy."

"But you're willing to put in the time and work just for him," Rex added.

Rex said that? Marla was about to give him grief for the comment when the doorbell rang. "Curtain going up!" she said on her way to answer the door. "Do your thing, kid."

"What a nice surprise," Kitty told their visitor in her warmest Kitty voice as Marla led him to the kitchen. The fluster had vanished.

"Here, take my seat," Rex told the newcomer, vacating his stool and moving to lean against the wall in a corner.

"Thanks, man," Hub Sherman replied, slipping in next to Marla. He wasn't the kind of guy she was expecting. Not particularly dashing. Tall with graying blond hair and even a bit of a paunch. The most striking part of his features was his gray-green eyes. Kind eyes, not the hard eyes Marla had pictured. And he appeared to be much younger than Kitty.

"You caught me, Hub." Kitty introduced Marla and Rex. "These two missed out on the pie I made earlier, so I'm making one for them tonight."

"She told me she'd used some new techniques she'd read about for making a flakier crust," Marla explained, "so she's demonstrating for us tonight."

"Looks like I arrived just in time," Hub said. Then he spotted the open sack of Prairie Harvest Flour. "And apparently you didn't need my addition." He set the flour he'd brought on the island counter. "But I hope I can stay. I'd really like to see how you put together the delicacy I tasted last night."

"Of course. Please do," Kitty said in a honeyed tone. "I've just started to put together the crust."

"Rex and I are waiting for our dinner to arrive, but you're

welcome to share it with us. We're having beef burritos," Marla said.

"Thanks, but I don't want to help myself to your dinner. Why don't I just order my own?" He didn't wait for them to respond but pulled his phone out and touched a number. He returned his attention to Kitty. "Please, continue with what you were doing."

To Kitty's credit, she kept her cool and continued to prepare the butter and shortening combo. Just as she was about to mix it in her blender, Hub jumped up. "Wait! That looks easy enough. Can I do it?"

"Be sure you ..."

He didn't give Kitty a chance to finish her warning but immediately claimed his place at the blender and flipped the switch. A shower of flour, butter and shortening shot out of the appliance and flew everywhere in the kitchen, caking not only the countertops and island but also the four of them.

"... place the lid on top," Kitty finished, seconds too late.

After that, no one said a thing for a few beats, all four of them too astonished to speak.

Hub took the worst of the deluge, his hair and clothes covered in the stuff, but Kitty's hair looked like it had gone white overnight.

"Omigosh! Sorry, everyone," Hub said weakly. "I had no idea that could happen."

"No kidding," Marla said, brushing flour off her top.

"That's not supposed to happen," Rex said. Trained to respond to emergencies, he was already pulling kitchen towels from drawers while Marla grabbed the roll of paper toweling. "There's a safety lock built in that won't let the motor engage if the lid's off. Unless that's an older model manufactured before that feature was added?"

"Older, like over thirty years?" Kitty asked, swiping flour

from under her eyes with a finger. "I think I got that thing for a wedding present in another life. I rarely use it." She retrieved a broom and dustpan, which she handed Hub. "Here. Start working on the floor." She fired up the hand vacuum and tackled another corner of the kitchen.

A half hour later, most of the debris had found its way to a couple of garbage bags. They took turns removing what they could from each other's hair, skin and clothes.

More than once, Marla and Rex exchanged looks, trying not to laugh. She wanted to say something to relieve the tension but left that to Kitty. This was her rodeo.

Kitty didn't disappoint. "And that, Hub, completes your first lesson in what not to do when preparing a pie crust."

Hub, apparently anticipating being banished from the kitchen and probably her condo, blinked until he realized he had already been forgiven.

"Good thing I brought that extra bag of flour, huh?" He laughed.

"Good thing you came here tonight not expecting a piece of pie," Kitty returned.

"I take it the kitchen is closed for the night?" Hub said.

"Good guess," Marla said.

That's when Marla and Rex's burritos arrived. Kitty had ordered one for herself too. The foursome rounded up plates, soft drinks and beers and headed for the dining room.

eighteen

. . .

The four of them dug into their meals and didn't say much the first few minutes other than to compliment the food. By silent agreement, Marla and Rex didn't mention their investigation, and Kitty picked up on that same vibe. After a bit, though, there was mainly silence.

Hub was the first to break it. "I'm really not the crazed lunatic you witnessed in the kitchen. Back me up there, Kitty," he said to his hostess.

"That is true," she replied. "For a few fleeting seconds, I didn't recognize you. You simply took over, which wasn't all that unusual"—she smiled back at him—"but not when it concerns baking. That kitchen persona was new."

"*Kitchen persona*? I like that. The thing is, I was hired for my present position because of my great promotional skills. And that's worked well for me. But my boss recently dropped a hint that for me to move up the ladder, he'd expect to see me demonstrating my culinary side. I guess I sort of mentioned that in my interview with him a million years ago. I forgot all about it. He didn't."

"What exactly is your *culinary side*?" Marla asked, recalling a few occasions long ago when she'd augmented her own credentials when auditioning for a part. Not smart. Most had come back to bite her in the behind.

"Prairie Harvest Flour was originally family-owned. Although it went public long ago, family members are still on the board. They take great pride in the large variety of baking goods that result from their product. I, uh, embellished my resume just a tad in order to enhance my chance of getting hired."

"And now the white lie has come home to haunt you?" Rex said, maintaining a straight face.

"He believes I'm a world-class baker and expects me to show him my stuff in the near future. That's why I've been so involved in this pie-baking contest and why I've been so interested in your pie-baking skills, Kitty."

Kitty set her half-eaten burrito back on her plate, her chin jutting out. "That's why you've been seeing me?"

He reached across and patted her hand. "Not the only reason. You're quite an interesting woman, Kitty Lovejoy. Not to mention being attractive and funny. But it hasn't hurt that you've told me you could bake a pretty good pie."

Kitty began to laugh so hard she had to cover her mouth with her hand. "Oh, Hub, you poor mistaken dummy."

Her changed attitude startled him. "Huh?"

Marla and Rex observed this exchange, trying hard not to burst out laughing themselves, but this was Kitty's show. They waited for her to explain.

"You're not the only one trying to impress someone else with your baking skills. I haven't baked a pie since I was working for a Girl Scout badge as a preteen. Marla's the pie baker in our family. And it was Marla and Rex who made the apple pie you raved about last night."

Hub sought out Marla and Rex. "Is that true?"

"It was a group effort," Rex replied. "Kitty handled the filling."

Hub took a moment to absorb this twist. "You did this just to impress me?" he asked Kitty.

She glanced at Marla. Surely she wasn't seeking her advice? No, Kitty could hold her own, and she knew it. This was more a silent apology for dragging them into this situation. "You find that hard to believe? You're not just an attractive man, Hub. You're fun to be with. And ... several years younger than me." She let him make what he would of that last statement.

Marla studied what was left of the burrito on her plate, resisting the urge to gaze at her sister. She hadn't believed Kitty had spoken the obvious out loud. Pretty smart of her. Throw down the gauntlet for Hub. It was up to him how to respond.

She tried to think of a plausible way she and Rex could get out of there and avoid this private scene, but nothing came to mind.

Hub came to their rescue. "Bet you two had no idea what you signed on for when you agreed to help Kitty with her pie making."

"I get the feeling we're not quite done yet," Rex said, man to man.

That was news. What had she missed, or was this a guy thing?

"You're sharp, man," Hub said to Rex. "I, uh, need your help. Based on what Kitty just said, from all of you."

Now Hub wanted to learn the ins and outs of pie baking? "Okay? Why don't you tell us how we can help," she said.

He leaned forward and folded his hands on the table. "I need to provide my boss with evidence of my baking skills when he's in town. I can't just present him with pies and cakes. He'll want to see me make them. Teach me, please."

Rex spoke before Marla could. "Sorry, man, but Marla and I are tied up in another matter at the moment which takes precedence over your career aspirations. You'll have to learn what you can from Kitty."

"Me?" Kitty replied, sounding clueless. Then she must have realized what a powerful position that put her in as far as her continuing relationship with Hub Sherman. "Uh, well, of course I'm at your service, Hub. But pie making isn't a skill you acquire overnight. We can use my kitchen or yours, but this will require at least three sessions. Do you have the time?"

Hub leaned over and put an arm around her shoulders. "I'll make time. But do you? I don't want to keep you from the rest of your life."

Marla listened, fascinated by this mating dance. At least that's what it was with Kitty. Her mind wasn't made up about Hub yet.

"I'll have to rearrange a few things, but I think that's possible. I want to do whatever I can to help you impress your boss. Marla and Rex can give me pointers when they're not off investigating the murder."

Hub swiveled his head their direction. "Murder? You guys are cops?"

Marla shot Kitty the evil eye, but the ship had already sailed. She suspected Kitty had done it on purpose, to make herself look good in his eyes. Like teaching him how to bake wasn't enough.

Rex handled this one. "I'm a former cop. Marla and I are consulting with the police on a homicide. That's all we can say. I'm sure you understand."

"Sure, man. Wow, I had no idea the two of you were into that stuff. I thought you were a TV star, Marla."

"I am, but my former role as a PI seems to have put me in

good stead with the locals, including the police. We've been giving Kitty pointers on our breaks."

"Impressive. Wait. This homicide you've been investigating? That wouldn't be Eloise Wallace, would it?"

Marla and Rex sat forward simultaneously. "It might be," Rex said before Marla confirmed it. "Why do you ask?"

"I've been so busy with this pie-baking contest, I hadn't paid much attention to it, but I knew her. I've done business with her company. In fact, she's the one who suggested the pie event."

"I thought that was your brainchild," Kitty said.

"The idea of Prairie Harvest Flour sponsoring some type of event that highlighted the product was, but like I told you, baking has never been my forte. So I went to her for ideas. It probably seems to you that a contest built around pie baking was a no-brainer, but until she suggested it to me, I couldn't see the light."

"When did you see her last?" Rex asked, slipping into interview mode. Marla couldn't blame him. They'd stumbled onto a veritable witness who knew their victim from a different perspective.

Hub rubbed his cheek. "Let me think. We met a couple months ago to discuss my ideas for my event, but now that I recall it, I saw her briefly just two weeks ago at the kickoff party. That's where I met you, Kitty."

"Did you meet her at that party?" Marla asked Kitty. Surely she would've said something, wouldn't she?

"I don't think so. I would have told you guys if I had."

Marla nodded, softening her tone. "Thanks. Just asking."

"What can you tell us about her, Hub?" Rex asked.

Hub sat back. "I get the feeling what has been a friendly dinner discussion just changed to a police interview."

Rex smiled back at him. "Yeah, I guess it does seem that way. We've been so focused interviewing the people she was with just prior to her death, we got excited to find someone outside that group who could give us a different viewpoint."

"I can't really help you there," Hub replied. "I only saw her a few times when we discussed the pie thing. That was all business. We met less than thirty minutes each time. She was friendly but not overly." He paused as if trying to remember more.

"What aren't you telling us, Hub?" Marla asked, picking up on his hesitation.

"I don't want to come across as an egotist if I tell you," he said.

"We're past that point," Kitty threw in. She left interpretation of her remark open.

"During the first ten minutes of my meeting with her, Eloise was sizing me up. Reading my eyes, my expressions, my body language. We were both promoters; it's what we do when assessing a client. Apparently that brief analysis told her I might be more amenable to the suggestions of a younger staffer, a younger female staffer. Did I say 'suggestions'? In plainer language, I meant someone who trades business favors for sex. Which I'm not! And it still rankles that she saw me like that, because I don't recall giving any indication I was one of those. If she hadn't already given me some great advice, I would've sought help elsewhere.

"Anyway, she called in her assistant and introduced us, at which point she turned my project over to her, saying outright she thought the young woman could meet my needs better than her. She even arched an eyebrow as she said it, just in case I'd missed her subtext. Then she even proposed the two of us discuss things over dinner that night."

"What was the name of this assistant?" Rex asked.

"Chloe," Hub said immediately. "I remember because it was distinctive, plus she gave me her card before I left."

"Did I understand you to infer Eloise was ready to prostitute this young woman?" Rex asked.

"You cut right to the chase, don't you?" Hub replied. "Yes, that's what she attempted. I thanked her for the offer but declined in no uncertain terms. I said I wanted to deal directly with her. She got the message and didn't push further. I don't do business that way." That last part was intended for Kitty.

Marla wanted to hear more. "Tell us more about Chloe. How did she react to her boss's offer?"

"For one so young and seemingly innocent, she was also smooth. As soon as Eloise assigned her to my project, she acted like that was the best of ideas and smiled invitingly. Except ..."

Marla couldn't wait for him to finish. "Except what?"

He scratched his head. "Give me a moment. There was something off about that scene." He massaged the back of his neck. Thought some more. "It happened so quickly, I almost missed it. She gave Eloise this look. She was standing sideways to me, which was why I wasn't sure I'd actually seen it. Not exactly an eye roll, but her eyes narrowed and hardened. But it was gone in a flash. Next, she swiveled to face me, all smiles. Like she lived to meet my needs."

"Do you remember anything else?" Rex asked.

Hub shook his head. "Nothing more comes to mind. Was any of that helpful?"

"It could be. We can't say much more at this point."

"I didn't consider myself her friend, but she did help me see my way through this project. She didn't deserve to die, so I wish you both well with your investigation."

"Thanks," Rex said. "If you think of anything else, give me a call." He pulled one of his cards out of his pants pocket. Then he morphed into Mr. Charm. "Marla and I will give Kitty as much time as we can spare to get you ready for your boss."

Rex's return to dinner companion didn't seem to faze Hub,

who turned to Kitty. "Let me know what ingredients and equipment you need and I'll order it delivered here, if you don't mind."

Kitty took a moment to snap back to reality. "Uh, sure, Hub. I'll put the list together tonight. We can start tomorrow or the day after. Just let me know."

nineteen

. . .

After dinner, Marla and Rex excused themselves and returned to his condo, leaving Kitty and Hub to process all that had taken place in the last few hours. They had their own thoughts to process.

"I continue to marvel at what a small world this is," Marla said as she sipped a glass of red wine.

Rex seated himself next to her on the sectional. "The fact that Hub Sherman knew our victim? That's on me. I should've realized there might be a connection, knowing they were in the same business."

"Don't be so hard on yourself. Kitty's been pretty choosy what she's told us about the guy. All we knew about was his connection to that flour company. Instead, focus on what we just learned about the relationship between Eloise and Chloe. What we suspected about that free lodging at the new apartment is probably true. Eloise was pimping Chloe. Chloe knew it and didn't like it. But she went along with it anyhow. Her motive for murdering her boss just got stronger."

"I thought I've taught you not to jump to conclusions immediately." He held up a hand. "It's likely, but we need to be sure."

"I know. I haven't jumped completely. Maybe just a short hop. So how do you propose we prove it?"

"Time to get them to start turning on each other," Rex said. "This could get ugly. Hope you have the stomach for it."

Marla recalled her early years on stage. She'd had to learn fast that not everyone told the truth or had her best interests at heart. She'd been so excited when she got her first part in an off-off-Broadway play because it meant she could begin to replenish her diminishing bank account. Then the show closed after two nights. The backers disappeared, and she never saw a penny of what was owed her. She'd had to pawn a ring given to her by her grandmother just for grocery money.

"Survival in the entertainment industry is not meant for the faint of heart," she told Rex. Loyalty was a treasured quality in the industry, because it was so easy to turn on friends when parts, money or celebrity were up for grabs. And though she tried not to go there, even as recently as last year that lesson kept repeating itself. She'd trusted the *Carruthers* showrunners to honor her contract and keep her in the role of Letitia Carruthers, and look how that had turned out. "Are you suggesting if we want to know about the real Chloe, we start with Tanner?"

"You read my mind," he said, patting her on the back.

"But rather than ask Chloe her opinion of Tanner, why don't we switch it up with Nell? We ask Nell about Grace and Grace about Brecken."

"That leaves asking Brecken about Tanner. Does he know him that well?" Rex asked.

"They've been playing on the same team a while. We'll just have to find out."

"Thanks for meeting me here," Tanner told them when he greeted them at a coffee shop near his apartment the next morning. "I felt the walls coming at me when we met at my place yesterday."

"This shouldn't take as long today," Rex told him. "We got most of your background information yesterday. Have you had a chance to reflect on how you described Chloe Reardon?"

"You mean, do I want to revise what I told you after thinking overnight about my interview with you? No. I actually fixed myself a champagne cocktail to celebrate having had the nerve to speak my mind for once. I wouldn't change what I told you."

"The Chloe we interviewed appeared to be young and innocent, almost naive. That's a far cry from the devious woman you described. Was she playing us?" Marla asked.

"That's for you to decide," he replied. "But since you said, 'appeared to be young and innocent,' that makes me think you saw it too. She trades on her youth, and Eloise bought it. Not that she didn't see through it, but Chloe's seeming innocence allowed Eloise to be the self-centered control freak she was. Some clients like the wide-eyed sweetness thing. Makes them feel they're not the self-aggrandizing bullies they really are. Eloise was smart enough to realize she couldn't fit that mold but wanted to cater to it, so she was mentoring Chloe for that role."

"Are you saying that Chloe wasn't unaware that Eloise was using her, forcing her to use her innocence with clients?" she asked.

"Exactly."

"How do you know?" Rex asked. "Did she ever tell you what she was up to or complain about Eloise's treatment?"

"No, she would never confide like that to me. She marked me as the one to shut out from the first day of her internship. I was too flattered to realize then that she was playing me. She kept asking me what I thought about this and how I'd deal with that.

More than once she thanked me for giving her the 'inside track.' She even batted her eyes once or twice and touched my forearm like we were confidantes."

"We hear you, Tanner, but that's just your interpretation of her actions. What solid evidence do you have that she's not so innocent?" Marla asked.

Tanner started to respond then stopped. "Why are you giving Chloe so much attention?" He stopped again. "Do you think she killed Eloise?"

"We didn't say that, but you have. Our job is to test out your opinion," Rex said.

Tanner sipped his macchiato, considering. "I guess I understand. I thought I had been giving you evidence."

"You've made a good start. But we need to know actual things she said or did, especially if you've got any proof," Marla told him.

"But that's the problem, what I've been saying about her. She's smart enough not to provide hard evidence."

"Maybe if we asked you a few questions?" Rex asked.

Tanner put his cup down. "Ask away."

"Let's start at the beginning," Rex began. "Tell us about the first time you ran into Chloe. What did she say? How did she introduce herself?"

"Actually, it was Eloise who introduced us. They'd just concluded the meeting where Chloe had accepted Eloise's offer of a paid internship. It was supposed to be for her next-to-last semester of school, but Eloise extended it through the second semester. Chloe smiled a lot but didn't say much. That's when Eloise announced I'd be moving to a different desk location so that Chloe could take mine. At least I got to keep my desk. I held my peace and didn't protest, knowing it would do no good once Eloise made up her mind. But as they were moving on from me I heard her say to Chloe, 'Good idea seating you close to me so we can work closely.' Chloe shot me this Cheshire Cat look that let me know she'd engineered the move."

"You're saying that Chloe was manipulative right from the start?" Marla asked.

"It's not the kind of hard evidence you want because it only involved Chloe, me and Eloise, but that should tell you how it was from the start."

"Did anyone else observe your interactions with Chloe?" Rex asked.

"It was mainly the four of us in the office, so eliminating Eloise and Chloe, that only leaves Nell. You should ask her directly what she recalls about working with Chloe, but one incident comes to mind that involved both Nell and me. You probably heard how Eloise was always pushing the limits with finances. Besides giving more and more of my work to Chloe, Eloise also turned over more and more financial tasks to her, not that Chloe was supposed to handle the accounting, but Eloise made her a go-between with Nell. Probably because she wanted to avoid having to constantly justify her spending to Nell. The thing is, Chloe quickly became another Eloise and challenged Nell at every juncture. More than once she said something like, 'Consider whatever I tell you to do the same as Eloise telling you to do it.' Nell responded once with, 'Don't try throwing your weight around with me. I'm the one who knows where all the bodies are buried around here. Eloise needs me.' You'd think that would be enough to put Chloe in her place. 'We'll just see about that,' Chloe told her."

He paused, searched Rex's face. "Is that the kind of thing you needed to know?"

"Did you personally observe that particular scene?" Rex asked, not answering his question.

"Yes. I'd been talking to Nell when Chloe came up to her.

She didn't wait for me to leave before she delivered her message."

"Okay, thanks. We'll check that out," Rex said. "Anything else come to mind?"

Tanner took a few more sips of his beverage. "Maybe talk to Eloise's ex, Brecken. He and Eloise may not get along all that well, but that hasn't kept him from stopping by every so often. Not too long ago, he and Chloe were talking in our break room when I walked in. 'Are you sure you want to do that?' he said. 'It's free rent. Who would turn that down?' she replied. 'You can't believe it's really free,' he told her. 'What does Eloise expect in return?' That's when it got interesting. I was surprised she didn't wait for me to leave or suggest I get out of there, but she didn't. I'm guessing she didn't consider me any kind of challenge. 'What do you think? She's smart enough to realize she's past the age of properly handling her out-of-state visitors. She needs me.' What does that tell you?"

It told Marla a lot more than they got from Chloe. If Nell and Brecken confirmed what Tanner had just related, the young woman was not the innocent she tried to present to them. It didn't make her the killer, but it did suggest she'd been hiding her real self from them.

"Thank you. We'll add what you've told us to our notes."

"Yeah, thanks, Oliver," Rex said. "If anything else occurs to you ..."

"Get in touch. Got it," Tanner replied.

They grabbed their coffees to go and left Tanner to finish his macchiato back at the coffee shop.

"That was a great idea," Marla said once they were in the car. "Although it may be more difficult to get the rest of our suspects to rat out the others than it was with Tanner."

"True, but thanks to Tanner, all we have to do to get started with Nell and Brecken is to verify what he overheard. Then we take it from there."

twenty

. . .

Nell was in the middle of packing up the belongings of her late wife when they arrived at her house. "I thought I told you everything I knew yesterday. I certainly went on and on about my experience working for Eloise."

"And what you told us was very helpful," Marla said, keeping her tone amiable as they got started. "But we've gained a fuller picture of Mrs. Wallace's life since talking to you. We'd like to go over a few new points with you."

Nell gently set the box she'd been working on aside. "Okay, I get that. Eloise was a complicated woman with a complicated life. What else do you want to know?"

"When we talked to you earlier, you told us you confronted the victim on the pickleball court last Saturday after you'd learned that Chloe was now living rent-free in the apartment Eloise recently purchased. Tell us again how that happened," Rex said.

"I told you that I ran into Chloe quite by chance at the grocery store the day before. Apparently part of the deal was that she could live there rent-free as long as she kept the place stocked with food and drink for visitors, which was why she was there buying groceries. From the looks of her cart, she was spending almost as much there as she might have on rent."

"Could you describe her mood?" Marla asked.

"As I told you before, she was excited. So up that she had to tell me about her good luck even knowing how I felt about its purchase."

"Tell us a little more about that encounter," Marla continued. "You said you ran into her 'quite by chance.' When you think back on that meeting now, do you still believe it was accidental?"

Nell narrowed her eyes, crinkled her forehead. "That's an odd question. I just assumed that was the case. I was studying the fat content of various ice cream containers. Old habit I learned from Katharine. I do things like that since her death. Unconsciously mostly. I don't know if it is preventing me from moving on or not, but it makes me feel better. Anyway, I was engrossed looking at the numbers. She just seemed to show up at my side. 'What a surprise. I didn't know you shopped here,' she said. Now that I think back, I guess that was an odd statement, since the grocery store is just down the street from here."

"Had you ever seen her there before?" Rex asked.

"No. Both her old place and the new apartment are in St. Paul. Nowhere near Maple Knolls. I know because I dropped her off at the former once, and out of curiosity I'd driven by Eloise's new purchase."

"Did you comment on her being out of her area?" Marla asked.

"No. I was so overwhelmed to hear she was living there rent-free, my mind was completely on that. Her being out of her area is only hitting me now."

They were rounding the issue, trying not to put words in her mouth while they helped her remember.

"Are you saying it was a setup?" Nell asked, the direction of their questions dawning on her.

"That's for you to decide," Rex told her. "We don't want you to say or admit to anything you don't believe. Don't tell us what you think we want to hear. That will only deter us from finding the killer and possibly make things worse for you."

She seemed to think through his words. "Okay, then, it could have been a setup, since I'd never seen her at that store in the past, it was completely out of her way and she just showed up next to me. But if it was, then there's a different side of Chloe than I've seen before. No, that's not quite the case. I told you she came across as naive, but I also said I wasn't sure if that was the case. This makes me think the naivete is a cover."

"If that's the case," Marla said, "does that make you see other interactions you've had with her in a different light?"

"Do I think she was putting on an act for Eloise to suck up to her? Maybe, but that doesn't ring true for Eloise. She wasn't one to be taken in by anyone. But for such unremarkable talent, it was remarkable how Chloe was only supposed to intern for a semester and then stayed on not only for another semester but got herself hired full time without any apparent recruitment process."

She stopped, seemed to be thinking back over the last two years. Marla and Rex gave her the time to do it.

"Eloise had to have been on to her, and if that was the case, then she sanctioned Chloe's act. At least around the rest of us." She continued to think out loud. "All that being the case, maybe she and Chloe planned that chance meeting at the grocery store." She returned to thinking. "What did they hope to gain from it? I get that far in going back over this, but I can't see beyond."

"What was the result of seeing her?" Rex asked.

"I got angry and let it build overnight to the point of having it out with Eloise on the court. But why would she want to engineer that? Did she want me to quit the team?"

"Would quitting have played into Eloise's plans?" Marla asked, unable to figure out that one herself.

"Only if she planned to replace me with someone else. I suppose that could have been Chloe, but she's had some secret commitment on Saturdays, so Eloise hadn't pushed her to join the team like she did with the rest of us."

Suppose this one time Eloise had been unaware of her protégé's action. Suppose Chloe deliberately riled up Nell to foment another blowup. Could she have been setting Nell up as chief suspect in Eloise's murder? Marla filed that thought away to discuss later with Rex. For now, they still had one more point to cover.

"If what you're supposing about Chloe has been the case, were there other times she might've tried to set you up at work?" Marla asked.

"There could have been. I've never considered Chloe in that light. Could I think about that a bit, like overnight? Or—wait. You know something else, don't you? Why don't you just come out and ask me?"

"We can't lead you, Ms. Hampton," Rex said. "Otherwise, whatever you tell us might not hold up in court if it ever came to that."

She nodded. "You mean, I might have to testify someday?"

"It's a possibility," Rex replied.

"That's scary. For me. I'm not good at speaking in public."

"All you'd have to do is answer some questions and tell the truth," he reassured her.

"And that may not even happen," Marla added.

"How about we ask you this," Rex continued. "Do you recall any instances at work where Chloe expressed her opinion of your work in front of witnesses?"

"The only witnesses would have been Eloise herself and Tanner Oliver. I think Tanner was somewhere in the area a couple times when Chloe questioned my accounting skills."

"Do you recall what she said to you at those times?" Marla asked.

Her shoulders collapsed. "Not the exact words. More the gist of them, which was that whatever she told me to do, I should take as a direct order from Eloise. Told me, mind you. It seemed to me she was on a power trip that would soon be cut short once Eloise learned of it. But considering what we were just discussing, maybe Eloise was on to her all along, or even egging her on."

"Thank you," Marla said.

"Wait, something else occurs to me. Check with Brecken, Eloise's ex. I think he might have been around on one of those times when she was flexing her muscles."

"What was he doing there?" Rex asked. "Hadn't they been divorced for several years?"

"He used to hang around all the time when Grace still owned the company. Not so much since then, but he'd still pop by these last few years. I'd see him joking around with Chloe, generally when Eloise wasn't around."

"We were under the impression he and his ex-wife didn't get along that well," Marla said. "Why did he stop by, if that was the case?"

"You'll have to ask him. He borrowed money from Eloise's personal account more than once, so I guess he put up with her because of that. Although, if I recall, he and Grace were close when she was there."

They thanked Nell and let her get back to her difficult task. They were starting to put the pieces together after these second interviews. Just a few more and maybe they'd have it.

twenty-one

. . .

"So far, a successful morning," Rex said. "Kinda frightening what happens when you pit one suspect against another."

"It will be interesting to see if they come up with even more damning information once they have overnight to think about it," Marla replied.

"Back in the day, I saw that happen more than once with witnesses and suspects. They'd take away the feeling that we didn't suspect them. That they were working with us to nail the lawbreaker. And in so doing, they'd unload even more the next time we interviewed them, sometimes even at their own expense."

"Have you ever interviewed two suspects together?" she asked.

"No, but the occasion never arose. It would be risky, if we did it. They could both clam up and we'd get nowhere."

"But isn't that what we've seen so far from Grace and Brecken?" she said. "They've come close to telling a little more about the other and then they've hung back. If we could break one, maybe the other would feel compelled to one-up them."

A few beats went by while he considered what she proposed they do. "Okay," he said finally. "Let's give it a try. We can always separate them if the interview is going nowhere or do follow-up interviews with each."

They met within the hour at Grace's house. Brecken had offered the use of his landscaping office, but Grace's house offered more privacy.

Brecken greeted his hostess formally and took a seat across the room from where she sat until Rex asked them to sit closer together.

"Uh, sure," Brecken said. "Grace and I know each other from way back."

"Let's start there," Marla said. "You touched on that in your first interview. Please, each of you tell us a little more about how you know each other. Why don't you start, Grace?"

Grace had been staring at her hands. Now she gazed directly at Marla and Rex. "We both grew up in this area and were in high school together, although Brecken is a few years older. I left town for a number of years and didn't see him again until about nine years ago. That was a chance meeting at a local nursery, where he happened to mention both he and Eloise were on the job market again due to being laid off by their current employer. After that, after I hired Eloise, I saw him every so often when he'd be in the office or at a few social gatherings. I haven't seen him as much since I sold Essy, other than more recently when we both wound up on Eloise's pickleball team."

"How about you, Mr. Wallace? Is that a good summary of how you know each other?" Rex asked him.

Brecken didn't exchange looks with Grace but instead replied immediately. "Yes. I can't add anything."

They'd been expecting this. Time to throw them off. Marla took the lead. "It makes sense that you'd stop by to see your wife while you were still married, but you've been divorced for six years, Mr. Wallace. Yet we've heard you continued to drop by after that. What was the draw then?"

Brecken shot a brief glance in Grace's direction but quickly returned his gaze to Marla. He shrugged. "I don't know. Nothing in particular. I guess I got in the habit of dropping by every so often when I was still married to Eloise. Besides, they make pretty good coffee. Free coffee." He chuckled, attempting to dismiss the question.

Rex took his turn. "On those occasions when you 'dropped by,' who did you speak with?"

Another shoulder roll. "I don't recall specifically."

"Your ex?" Rex asked.

"Yeah, on occasion. We still had mutual business to discuss even after our divorce."

"And when you didn't have business to discuss with her?"

"Sometimes Nell, sometimes Grace. Why these questions? How are they related to Eloise's murder?"

"We're following up on points that didn't make much sense to us once we reviewed our earlier interview findings," Marla said. "The fact that you continued to stop by the office after your divorce sticks out to us. Getting a free cup of coffee doesn't explain it. There had to be a reason. That's all we're after."

"I already told you," Brecken said evenly, without adding anything further.

Marla continued to press, refusing to let Brecken wave off his visits. Letitia would sometimes embroider on the truth to convince a suspect to say more. She'd give it a try. "From what we've learned from others in the office, most of those visits involved Grace. In her office with the door closed," she said. "Do you and Grace have a closer relationship than you've let on?"

Brecken rose. "How dare you insinuate—"

"Just answer the question, Mr. Wallace."

Grace placed a hand on Brecken's forearm. "It's okay, Breck.

Don't feel you have to protect my honor." She switched her attention to Marla and Rex. "Brecken and I have developed a strong friendship over the years. Eloise picked up on it and made our lives miserable even after the divorce."

Finally! Marla hadn't been sure they'd ever get an admission out of either of them. "Are you telling us you've been lovers?" she asked. Personal, prying questions like that had arisen enough times in her *Carruthers* scripts that she was able to ask this one now without cringing at her own audacity.

"That's none of their business, Gracie," Brecken said, although he did retake his seat.

"Actually, it is," Rex replied. "Neither of you has been completely honest with us about your relationship. That makes us question everything else you've told us." He didn't add that the two of them being lovers upped their motives for murdering Eloise.

Grace took over for Brecken, whose indignation was still quite noticeable with his red face. "Breck and I were friends in high school. We didn't date, but I hung out with his group of friends until he graduated. We stayed in touch after I left town. We renewed our friendship after Eloise came to work for me. We were just friends for a few years, while he and Eloise were still married. We each had our problems with her, which we shared with each other. We came close to crossing the line before the divorce but held back because we didn't want to make things worse for Breck.

"Eloise was okay with the divorce, but her ego couldn't accept the idea that he loved another woman. In the months just prior to the official split, she caught us together, not making love, but we were engaged in a deep, personal discussion. She threatened to make things more difficult for Breck. He'd already moved out of their house, but she wanted more alimony. She really didn't deserve any because she was making more money than he was at the time; I knew, because I was the one paying her.

"Within the year after the divorce, Eloise won the lottery. Up until then, she had been slowly taking over the company, and like I told you yesterday, I let her. She was smarter than me on the business end. She used some of her newfound wealth to buy her partnership. At least Breck was relieved from paying alimony from then on. But becoming my partner wasn't enough for her. In her eyes, I'd taken her man, even though she'd lost him long before that, so she set out to take Essy from me. She invested what remained of her lottery money and within a couple years was able to buy me out.

"Breck and I have continued to keep our relationship quiet. We've been together but not openly. She made it clear she could do us more harm if we made it public."

They'd found the mother lode. Or at least a huge vein.

"What further harm could she do to you at that point?" Rex asked.

Grace opened her mouth to reply but stopped and looked at Brecken. "She was threatening Breck at that point. I assumed she'd try to wreck his business. His landscaping company was finally gaining more clients. Essy is about information. There was no telling how she could use fake information to hurt him."

"Is that true, Mr. Wallace?" Marla asked.

He blinked like his mind had been elsewhere until the question was directed at him. "Uh, yeah. Eloise could be very vengeful. Since she mostly got away with it, it was wise not to tangle with her."

Interesting how he let Grace do the talking and didn't add much even though he had been the one his ex bullied.

Rex must've been thinking the same thing, because he asked another question. "How does what you both just told us about the victim's vindictiveness mesh with her giving you a loan just six months ago? She gave it to you, didn't she?"

"Yeah, she did," Brecken replied. "But it came with strings. I told you how the deal was that I'd join the pickleball team and if I left before I'd paid back the loan, the remainder of the loan plus a twenty-five-percent cancellation fee were due immediately. But her control didn't end there. She acted like she owned my business, forever putting down the various jobs we did around town. Even badmouthing my company to potential clients."

Brecken addressed the question this time rather than talking around it. But what a sick situation between the two former spouses. Marla had yet another question for him. "Your wife bought out Ms. Adamson four years ago. So why did you continue to stop by the Essy office even when Ms. Adamson was no longer there?"

"I've already answered that question," Brecken replied.

"Yes, but that was before we learned you and Ms. Adamson are lovers," Marla said. "Let's have one more try at it now that we know about your relationship."

Grace and Brecken exchanged looks. "My visits weren't as frequent as when Grace was there. In fact, I did it mainly for Grace. It's been difficult for her to let go of the company she built from nothing. I hardly spoke to Eloise at those times. Instead, it was mainly Nell I checked in with. Once Grace was out of there, Eloise turned the bulk of her ire on Nell. More recently until her wife's death, Nell struggled to stay on top of her work while she and Katharine dealt with her health. Grace didn't feel comfortable going there, so I took it upon myself to do it for her."

"What about Tanner and Chloe?" Marla went on. "Were you compelled to check in with them as well?"

"It's only been recently that Tanner complained about Eloise and felt comfortable sharing his concerns with me."

Had he deliberately not mentioned Chloe? "And Chloe?" Marla pursued.

"I spoke with her on occasion. She was and still is Eloise's strongest supporter. Grace and I have been concerned about Eloise's influence over her. She's so young and easily manipulated."

Rex didn't let that comment rest. "Interesting that you would describe Ms. Reardon that way, since others have suggested the naivete is an act."

"Tanner is jealous of Chloe since she appears to have taken his place as Eloise's main supporter. Of course he'd portray her that way. And Nell? Chloe has been trying to lighten some of her workload while Nell has been dealing with Katharine's health. It's understandable Nell might feel Chloe was invading her space," Brecken said.

Both explanations made a certain amount of sense. And Brecken jumped into his reply without hesitation. But did they ring true? Something they'd need to discuss later.

"Okay, we've been more than candid with you, but the fact that you're still talking to the two of us tells me you're no closer to finding Eloise's killer than you were when we first met. Perhaps a call to the Maple Knolls chief of police or even my state senator will speed things along," Brecken said, his tone becoming more belligerent.

No point responding to his taunt. "I think we're done here for now," Rex said. "Thank you both for meeting with us."

"We got a little more than we knew going in," Marla said once they had left the house.

"Thanks to Grace," Rex replied. "If we'd left it up to Brecken, we'd be no further ahead than we were going in. He clearly didn't want to say any more than he had before. And why?

Because there definitely was and is a relationship between the two of them. He hasn't been lying, but he's been holding back information we need to get further with this case."

"I still can't get past the fact he's been dropping by the Essy office every so often long after his divorce and then after Grace sold the business to Eloise."

"You don't buy his reasons?" he asked.

"Not so much that I don't buy them, I just suspect there's more there he's not telling us. He may not be telling Grace, either, or she might have broken in to augment his response."

"Any idea how we can get him to tell us?"

"It wasn't until we asked why he continued to visit Essy even after Grace was no longer there that he gave up any information. So we have to find more evidence to throw at him about those visits. We've gone back to Tanner and Nell but not Chloe. Knowing now that she's not that naive, we should talk to her again about her time as an intern and then as Eloise's assistant. Maybe she'll reveal something we can use to trip him up."

"Good plan, but first, let's take a break. I need to process all we've learned this morning," Rex said.

twenty-two

. . .

"I feel the need to get away from all this so we can clear our heads," Rex said. "Where do you want to go?"

"Can we skip your condo or Kitty's this time and go somewhere else?" Marla asked. "I don't have a specific location in mind, but I'd like to get out of the vehicle and walk around a bit. No heavy hiking but a chance to get some fresh air. By water, if possible."

"Then let's head to Riley Lake. It's between here and Maple Knolls and should be fairly unoccupied this time of day."

"Great plan. Can we stop somewhere and grab sandwiches or something first? I didn't have much for breakfast because I was so intent on our upcoming interviews."

"I'm with you there. A bowl of cereal only lasts so long in my stomach," he said.

Twenty minutes later, they sat at a picnic table not far from the lake eating grilled chicken wraps they picked up on the way.

"I've never been to this lake before," Marla said after she'd swallowed her first bite. "In fact, I didn't even know it was here."

"It's one of the area's secrets. I've brought my grandkids here on occasion, although of course, they prefer the swimming area on the other side."

"I'm more used to swimming pools in California. But as a child, our parents took Kitty and me to one of two resorts where we'd spend a week every summer," Marla told him, remembering times she'd forgotten."

"Is that where you learned how to water ski?"

"Oh, right, I mentioned before how I was able to get out of the water and then frightened myself with the speed."

"Do you still swim?"

"I have a pool at my house in California that's pretty much *de rigueur* out there. When we were shooting, I'd put in a few laps most days to wind down, unless we shot too late. But I haven't been in the water much since being let go."

"Maybe you should try it again at the Rambling Meadows pool?" he suggested. "It's indoors, which is *de rigueur* in Minnesota." He smiled.

"That sounds like a great idea if this case goes another day. Being here will help me unwind for now."

"I might even join you. It's been a few weeks since I hit the water."

They finished their wraps and disposed of their garbage in a nearby trash receptacle. "I'm ready to discuss our morning," she said.

"Let's walk and talk," Rex said. "Start with Tanner."

"No love lost there between him and Chloe. Or ..."

"Does Tanner protest too much?" he asked.

"That thought hadn't occurred to me until just now. I haven't even been convinced he's heterosexual. But if he is, I guess it's an angle we should consider. But if that's the case, why would he be doing his best now to implicate her or at least to portray her as a schemer?"

"That touchy-feely stuff is your area, Marla."

She pulled up, kicked at a tuft of grass while her brain worked through the labyrinth of that possibility. "If he's got a thing for her and yet he's been putting her down to us at every corner, that suggests a thwarted lover seeking revenge."

He stopped beside her. "We need to find out if he ever came on to her and she turned him down. File that one away as a question for Chloe."

They were making their way along a footpath that in twenty feet turned and ran parallel to the lake. The early fall wind danced with her hair, lifting it and flinging strands every which way. The sun glowed a brilliant yellow and warmed her face.

The lake was a bit choppy due to the breeze, the color a slate blue. It called to her. Not hypnotically like it wanted her to walk right in, but invitingly, just urging her closer. It seemed to whisper that it had the answers she was seeking, if only she paid attention. She pressed on, intent on getting closer.

"But even if Tanner was magnifying Chloe's faults to get back at her, that doesn't mitigate what we learned from Nell," she said more to herself than to Rex.

"There is that. I didn't get the impression she was out to get her younger co-worker. She only saw that run-in at the grocery store as planned after our questions took her to that conclusion." He paused and sniffed. "Smell that? Fall is coming soon. My favorite season. Do the leaves even turn in California?"

"Depends on the tree and your location," she replied. "If you're up in the higher altitudes, it's almost like being here in Minnesota. Almost but not quite." Fall. The typical beginning of a new season on the major TV networks. Once again, she wouldn't be part of it. The pain was still there, but a day like this and sharing this investigation with Rex helped.

"Back to Chloe and her co-workers." A new thought hit, although it had been right there under the surface all along. "Actually, Tanner is her only co-worker now that Eloise is dead.

And Chloe is the designated beneficiary. No more Eloise with the business sense, Nell as the financial gatekeeper, and the creativity of Grace is long gone." She turned to Rex. "Surely that young woman doesn't think she can run the whole show?"

"It's possible, but I don't see her as the one coming up with the idea. That would've been Eloise, except she got the short straw in the proposition."

"Do you suppose that was the idea, only it backfired on Eloise?"

"Then who? Is there someone off the page we don't know about?" Marla asked.

"It's possible. Something to keep in mind, but it doesn't ring true for me."

Marla thought back over everything else they'd learned that morning. "If there is another puppet master, Grace would be the most likely candidate, except she appears to have had little contact with Chloe. She was no longer there when Chloe first showed up. Without coming right out and saying it, Nell resented what she considered Chloe's interference with her responsibilities."

"Which leaves Brecken," Rex said. "It might explain his still popping by even after Grace was gone."

"Perhaps, but why? Surely he doesn't have some master plan to take over Essy? Unless he was doing it for Grace?" She waved it off. "No, no. That's too Machiavellian for a guy who so far has come across as pretty simple."

"I think this break is over," she said, pivoting. "Time to talk to Chloe again."

"What about Liz Parsons?" he asked. "I didn't think we'd dismissed her as a suspect just yet."

"Well, no, but we weren't able to come up with a very good motive for her."

"All the more reason to keep talking to her," he said.

She cocked a brow in his direction. "What aren't you telling me, Rex? What do you know about Liz Parsons?"

"Just a need to be thorough and interview her a second time like the others. I'm not convinced she stayed in touch with Eloise because she wanted her help launching her fashion business."

Though she had a great time arguing with Rex, he knew his stuff. She'd learned not to doubt him. "Okay. Who knows? Maybe she has some insights about Chloe."

They were no sooner in the SUV when their phones buzzed. Goodhue texted them that he was forwarding the financial info on their six suspects plus Eloise Wallace. He told them he'd meet them at five at Rex's condo to get an update. It wasn't a suggestion.

"Looks like we've got our work cut out for us for the rest of the afternoon," Rex said. "Not only do we have to meet with Liz and Chloe, we also have to absorb what's in these reports and do whatever follow-up they may suggest."

They stayed there at the lake reading. Eloise had a couple million in her personal account. She'd paid Grace five million for Essy four years ago. She appeared to be living on her lottery winnings since buying the firm, not paying herself a salary but reinvesting her share of the profits back into the company. As Nell had complained, she'd paid $1.5 million for the new apartment.

Nell received a fifty-thousand-dollar payout even though she was fired. She was still paying down the mortgage on the home she and her late wife owned. Katharine Riley's life insurance was still in probate. Once it passed, Nell would receive two hundred thousand.

Grace owned her house outright. She'd been living on part of the money she received from the sale of Essy but still had over four million in the bank.

Brecken's personal bank account was a little over five thousand. Six months ago, he'd received one hundred thousand dollars from Eloise, which he'd quickly placed in his company account. Other than the specifics, they knew most of this. What they didn't know was that beginning eight years ago, he paid a thousand dollars every three months into an account named Carmen. Those payments lasted about three years. There was no explanation of what Carmen was or why the payments stopped.

Liz's financial history matched what they'd learned earlier about her various employers including her time in the Netherlands. About eleven and a half years ago, she received a life insurance check for a million dollars. Not too long after that she sold the house in Georgia for another million. She bought her condo for six hundred thirty thousand. Over the next few years, she'd laid out close to seventy-five thousand renovating the condo and another fifty thousand on a new car. Another hundred thousand had been laid out in incidental expenses. She'd invested about a hundred thousand setting up her business as a financial consultant, leaving well over a million dollars in her account.

"Maybe it was a good idea to check in with Liz next," Marla said. "I'd like to hear why she thought she needed Eloise's money to finance her fashion business. Her report doesn't show any of her own investment in that plan."

Tanner appeared to be living hand-to-mouth. His salary, currently ninety-three thousand, barely covered food, rent, car payments and incidentals. His bank account showed a little over twelve hundred dollars.

For only being a year out of college, Chloe's financial situation was more stable than Tanner's even though she was making only sixty thousand in salary. Her college expenses had been paid off by an inheritance from her mother, who died during Chloe's first year of college. To get the full story, they would need the mother's financial picture. A single mother, she'd been a paralegal until a few months before her illness. Chloe had around ten thousand dollars in her bank account.

"Chloe appears to have benefited from the death of, first, her mother and now, from what we learned from Boris Doppler, from Eloise's death," Marla observed. "Her financials don't tell us much."

"Let's track down Liz first and then Chloe," Rex said. "Then double back to my place to meet with Goodhue."

twenty-three

. . .

*L*iz Parsons agreed to meet them at her condo in a half hour. She was just finishing up a client meeting in St. Paul, and that was the soonest she could get there.

"I'm curious what more you could possibly want to know from me," she began once they'd entered her domain.

"Mainly follow-up, Liz," Marla told her. "To make sure we understood what you told us."

"Plus, we've learned a few more things about your relationship with the deceased since then we want to clarify," Rex said.

"Do tell," Liz replied. "This should be interesting."

"You told us you knew Eloise Wallace from way back. How far back and in what capacity?" Marla asked.

"Is that important? Like I said, it was ages ago."

"Humor us," Rex said.

"We were in college together."

Was Liz deliberately trying to remain obtuse? "Together as in the same school, the same classes or the same room?" Marla asked.

Liz took her time answering. "We were roommates our sophomore year."

"How did you get along?" Rex asked.

"You know how it is," she replied. "Sometimes it clicks with roomies, and sometimes you have to try harder to get along. Eloise and I were in that second category. She borrowed my things without asking. Not just clothes. My cosmetics. My books. My boyfriends." Her volume dropped off with that last one.

"What did you do about it?" Marla asked.

"At first, I confronted her. She either denied having taken whatever it was or came up with some lame excuse, like she thought I'd given her my permission to use it. As time went by, and the denials and excuses continued, I stopped confronting her directly. Those personal items I really didn't want her to touch I hid. Although I couldn't do that with boyfriends."

"And she helped herself to someone you really cared about?" Marla guessed.

Liz bowed her head. "Yes. After that, I put in for a room transfer."

"How did that go?" Marla asked, still having to drag it out of her.

"She found out. One of her friends worked in the housing office and told her. She confronted me about it and said I was making her look bad to other students. Can you imagine? Me. Even then, I came clean with her and told her why I wanted out of there. She had the gall to deny any of those incidents happened, and since there were no other witnesses, she more or less got away with it. I kept my distance from her the rest of the time I was at school."

"Thank you. That wasn't so hard, was it?"

Liz looked away from them. "I didn't want you to think I carried those feelings against her all these years."

"So it would look like you had a motive to kill her?" Rex asked.

"Well, yes."

"That brings us to the near present," Marla said. "To four months ago when you ran into her again after all these years. Or had you seen her again prior to that meeting?"

"Didn't see her, although I did hear about her a few times."

"You told us that initially you didn't want to join the pickle-ball team but changed your mind when you decided she might be able to help finance your venture into fashion design. Is that correct?"

"Yes."

"Why did you need her financing when you already had over a million in the bank?" Marla asked.

"You ... you checked my bank account?"

"Of course. You didn't think we would?" Rex asked.

"Well, no. I didn't kill her. I thought that would be obvious to you, too, and you would have already dismissed me as a suspect."

"We're not quite there yet," Marla replied. "Please, answer my question."

Liz puckered her lips while she patted her legs with her hands. Seeking a credible reason why she was still with the team? "Okay, I'll tell you the truth. It just doesn't make me sound very nice."

"Just give us the truth."

"That day I ran into her, all those memories from thirty-some years ago came flooding back, the smugness, the fake interest, the ego. I tried to dismiss my feelings and remind myself I was better than that, better than her. She kept going on about how successful she was and how much my consulting business could benefit from her brilliant mind. I was so ready to get out of there and never see her again.

"At some point, I must have mentioned I lived at Rambling Meadows, which is when she invited me to join her pickleball team. My first thought was to turn her down point-blank, but then I realized she'd only invited me because she wanted to play on our courts. Once again, she was using me. Three decades of putting all her abuses behind me suddenly disappeared, and it was like I was back in college again. Only this time I wanted to get the better of her. So I joined the team to get the inside scoop on who Eloise now was so I could make her life as miserable as she once made mine."

She stopped and held her upturned palms out surrender-style. "That's why I joined the team. Not very high-minded, but some wound deep within me that I thought had healed years before reared its ugly head."

Not what Marla was expecting to hear, but it made a certain amount of convoluted sense. "So?" she asked. "Did you succeed?"

Liz thought about it. "In a way," she replied. "It soon became clear that I wasn't the only one who had issues with the woman. Her ex was there because he owed her money, a debt she never failed to mention along with criticizing his play as her partner. Her ex-partner who she'd bought out years before under what I learned had been a very acrimonious relationship was still hanging around for reasons I couldn't understand. Her accountant was always bringing up financial issues that should have been left at work. And you witnessed that final blowup on the court, Marla, even after she'd been fired two weeks before. And finally, there was her assistant, who she was constantly chiding.

"All I had to do was insinuate myself with each of them to stir the pot. And since you've interviewed all of them at least once, you already know even that wasn't necessary. Hate, the need for revenge and fear were already festering beneath the surface with all of them. But I never, believe me, realized one of them would kill her."

"That's it?" Rex said, unconvinced. "You hung out with the

team for several weeks just to get back at a woman who took advantage of you over thirty years ago?"

"Yes. Haven't you ever put up with someone who has injured you just to find some sort of cosmic justice for yourself?"

Marla fought her impulse to gaze at Rex. Liz had unknowingly touched upon the bond that brought him into this investigative partnership.

Rex didn't respond.

"Anyway, that's my story," Liz said with finality.

"How long were you planning to stay with the team?" she asked.

Liz sat back and tilted her head to the side. "I hadn't decided yet, even though every Saturday I came home vowing they'd seen the last of me. The friction you witnessed on the court Saturday, Marla, was par for the course. They may not have gotten along with each other, but the soul-grinding put-downs she dished out to everyone were the one thing that bound them together."

"Can we assume the team is over now that the self-appointed captain is dead?" Rex asked.

"I guess so, although I haven't heard anything official. No one really liked the game or, well, liked playing on that team with her. I know I'm done, which means they won't have access to the Rambling Meadows courts."

"What about your fashion line?" Marla asked, not having forgotten Liz's original story. "You've had money in the bank for some time. Instead, you've continued to work as a consultant."

"You don't let anything get past you," Liz told her. "I told you about my hopes of designing fashions just to explain why I remained on the team."

"I'm disappointed. I was looking forward to seeing an example of your work," Marla replied.

"Really? It's not like I haven't thought about it, but I guess I, uh, have been afraid to try."

"You? You don't strike me as being afraid of anything, Liz," Marla said. "You have a diverse background, which includes well over a decade as a buyer for women's clothing. You know what the market wants, even if that was a few years back."

"If I did try my hand at design, would you be willing to look at my work and critique it?" she asked timidly.

"If you don't turn out to be the killer, yes, I'd be happy to," Marla told her.

Liz broke into smiles. "Then get ready to analyze. You've inspired me."

twenty-four

. . .

"I hope you were serious with that offer to help her," Rex said as they walked to his car. "She went from deflated, having to admit to her baser reasons for sticking with the team, to excited at the prospect of returning to her dream."

"I was serious, not that I could do much to help her with the LA market right now, but I'd like to see what she can do."

"Does that mean you're ready to dismiss her as the killer?" he asked.

"I'm about ninety-five percent there. There's always a slight chance we missed something that would have revealed her as our culprit, but I'm reasonably confident she's in the clear. Do you agree?"

"I wasn't tracking with her revised reason for sticking with the team," he replied, "until she made that statement about putting up with someone who injured you in the past. She had me pegged as far as my working for Goodhue is concerned."

"Except Goodhue never injured you. In fact, you told me the man saved your life when you were both on the St. Paul police force. That's why you agreed to help on the Elliot case, because you felt you owed him."

"Something I shared with you in confidence."

"A confidence I will continue to respect," she said.

"I agree with you about Liz not being our killer. For now, we set her aside and focus on the other five." He paused while they climbed into his car. "How would you like a Diet Coke before we tackle Chloe again?"

"Great idea! I could use an afternoon pick-me-up. But what about you? Since when are you into soft drinks?"

"I've been known to imbibe a few, although I prefer the lemony-lime variety."

A few minutes later, they sat sipping their beverages at the outdoor eating area of the mom-and-pop café they visited. They didn't discuss the case.

"Are you ready to talk about your attempt to produce a video yet?" Rex asked out of the blue.

He hadn't forgotten, yet he'd gone along with her request not to discuss it earlier. "It's amazing how you can file information away but never lose it."

"It's a talent," he replied.

She chuckled. "Talent. Interesting choice of words. Maybe I don't have whatever talent is needed for making a video, because my first attempt didn't go well. I wasn't prepared for that. It was a shock that my already damaged ego didn't need."

"What happened?"

"I was supposed to be describing how to bake an apple pie, Kitty's brainchild. I'd only been considering the idea of video-casting, but Kitty leapt on it as her way of getting me to help her relearn the process to impress Hub. I'd already baked a pie the day before, so the process was in my head. But once the camera was rolling, the words stuck in my head. Maybe it was too soon, since I'm still not clear what my concept should be, what message I want to get across. Can we table this discussion for now?" she asked, suddenly uncomfortable telling him any more about this issue.

"Sure. Maybe once we're further along with this case or afterwards. Or not. I wasn't prying. Just trying to understand what happened."

She nodded. "I get that. Sorry, Rex. Producing my own video should've been right down my alley, and it wasn't. I need to work past my embarrassment. Especially around you."

"Me?"

"Let's not get into that right now, okay?"

"Fine with me." He took her empty can and disposed of it along with his.

"Ready for the Chloe Reardon show?" he asked after he'd started the SUV.

"As ready as we can be with that young woman. At least we have more background with which to question her this time."

"I thought you might be back," Chloe said when they showed up at her door. "You knew before I did that Eloise had named me her beneficiary. Her only beneficiary. And you wanted to see if I'd known about her decision already."

"Actually, we felt that information should come to you from Mrs. Wallace's attorney. To make it official," Rex said. "Since you brought it up, did you know?"

"Not for sure. Eloise had hinted around about naming me more than once, but I didn't think she was serious."

"Why was that?" Marla asked.

"Eloise was like that. Saying things to see how you'd react, not necessarily meaning them. I learned that lesson early in my internship when she suggested I could raise my grade by working on weekends. So I did, but my grade didn't change. When I asked her about it, she acted like it had never happened or that I had misunderstood."

"Does that describe the rest of your work relationship with her?" Marla continued.

"Unfortunately, yes. Don't get me wrong. I liked her as a boss. She had me performing tasks it would have taken years to be assigned elsewhere. I just couldn't trust her."

"Now that you do know, what do you intend to do about your role in Essy?" Rex asked.

She leaned forward conspiratorially. "Just between us, I don't have the slightest idea. Like I said, I didn't believe her when she hinted around that someday the business would be all mine. And even if I had, who knew she'd be dead so soon?"

"You seem to have a different opinion of your former boss today than when we spoke yesterday," Marla said. "Is that because in the meantime you've learned she did follow through and name you beneficiary?"

"Perhaps. Maybe I was still in shock at her death, especially then, learning she'd been murdered."

"That's one of the reasons why we're back today, now that you've had a little more time to get used to the idea of her death," Rex said. "And we've learned some more about the deceased and those closest to her we'd like to ask you about."

She smoothed her knit top and returned an expectant smile. "Okay. What do you want to know?"

Rex started. "Did you and Mrs. Wallace ever discuss your role at Essy?"

"I'm not sure I understand your question. If you mean did we go over my job tasks, yes. Those kept changing the longer I was there. She gave me more responsibilities as she got more familiar with my performance."

"That's part of what I meant, but I was also getting at her expectations for you at Essy. Since she named you her beneficiary, that would suggest she saw you relieving her of more and more of her job duties. Like becoming her protégé?"

"Oh, that kind of thing," she replied. "Yes. I learned long ago that she didn't trust many people, in particular Nell and Tanner. She never said as much, but I suspected she liked to 'play' with both of them by pitting me against them. I knew that put me into a less than amicable relationship with them, but I chose to go along with her desires. Call me ambitious. I don't mind. Ever since my mother's death, it's been just me. I have to take care of myself."

"It didn't bother you that Tanner and Nell didn't like you?" Marla asked, putting it to her directly.

"Of course it bothered me. I'm not unfeeling. But it was more important to get ahead in my job."

"What about more recently? Are you aware what she had in mind for you in your new

role as hostess in this apartment?"

Chloe pulled in her lips and gazed about the room. "Yes. She never put it in so many words, but it was clear she planned to trade on my youth and looks for business. But I knew what she intended. Be friendly with clients. Even have sex with them if necessary."

Marla hadn't been expecting her to admit as much. She must have realized they were on to her. "And you were ready to proceed with it?"

"No. I didn't know how I'd avoid following through when the time came. But the draw of this apartment had been too much to reject. I said yes thinking I'd figure out some way to get past the messy part down the road."

"Looks like that 'messy part' has already been avoided," Rex observed.

Her back went up immediately. "If you're saying that's because I killed her rather than go through with it, you're wrong. I didn't. The thought never even occurred to me."

"Maybe not directly, but what about your role in agitating

Nell enough for her to challenge Eloise on the court last Saturday?”

“I wasn’t there on Saturday. How could you say I agitated Nell?”

“Because you made a point of running into her at her grocery store the day before to brag about your new digs,” Marla said, taking over for Rex.

Chloe’s eyes went wide. “You know about that? What did Nell tell you?”

“She said that you came up to her all excited at your good fortune.”

Chloe nodded. “Okay, yes, that’s how it happened. But that wasn’t agitating her.”

“Really?” Marla said. “How was it you chose to go to a grocery store in Maple Knolls so far away from your new apartment?”

“I, uh, was in the area.”

“The day before you knew Nell would see Eloise at the pickleball match.”

“Pure coincidence.”

“And all the sudden you just showed up next to her?”

“Again, pure coincidence.”

Apparently Chloe was willing to admit to being ambitious and knowingly accepting her hostess role at the apartment, but she wouldn’t acknowledge trying to play Nell. How much would she tell them about Brecken?

“Let’s move on to another question,” Marla said. “We understand Eloise’s ex-husband dropped by the office every so often, even after their divorce. What can you tell us about those visits?”

“Not much. If I recall, they were divorced something like six years ago. That was long before I even interned there.”

“We realize that, but we’ve learned he continued to show up

even since you've been there. Did you talk to him at those times?"

She shrugged. "I guess so. He'd come in and pour himself a cup of coffee and then make his way around the place chatting with whoever was there. That was usually me, Tanner and Nell until she was fired. Sometimes he'd check in on Eloise, if she was there. I don't know what more I can tell you."

"What did you discuss when he talked to you?" Marla asked.

"I don't recall offhand. Nothing important enough to stick in my mind."

"Take a moment to reflect."

Chloe drew in a breath, eyes closed. "Almost without fail he'd ask how I liked it there and was Eloise treating me okay."

"How did you reply?" Marla asked.

"I always told him things were fine and that I enjoyed working for Eloise, even if one or the other wasn't the case that particular day. I got the feeling he was trolling for information he could use against her, and I didn't want to help him do that."

"What else did you talk about?" Rex asked.

"Is this really important?"

"Please, Chloe, just continue answering the question," Marla said, attempting to adopt Rex's firm, no-nonsense tone.

"All right, all right. Sometimes he'd ask how I was getting along with Tanner and Nell. Again, I always kept my responses upbeat and generic. A few times he asked if Eloise was using me to bug the other two. I played dumb on those, although once he'd planted that idea with me, I paid more attention to what Eloise asked me to do as far as they were concerned.

"Sometimes he got a little more personal. Never anything to creep me out. He was never that way. More like an interested uncle who cared about my welfare."

"What kinds of personal questions did he ask?" Rex asked.

She thought a bit. "How I liked college. That was during

my internship. Early on, he inquired about my parents. I told him that my mother had passed during my first year of college and that I never knew my father. My mother raised me by herself."

"Did he ask any follow-up questions about your mother?" Marla asked.

"Talk about getting personal. I don't know that I should have to answer these questions. Maybe I should ask an attorney to advise me."

"That's within your rights, but we are going somewhere with these questions," Rex replied, still in official mode. "We just have a few more."

"Okay, but if I start to feel even creepier answering, I will call someone. Anyway, yes, he expressed his sympathy when he learned my mother had died, although thinking back on it now, he didn't seem particularly surprised. Maybe Eloise told him. Then he wanted to be sure I'd been able to get through school without racking up a lot of debt. I told him that my mother had provided for that, although I suspected there was some relative who provided for her when she was alive because every so often she'd take me out to dinner or we'd have steak instead of hamburgers and salads. When I'd ask about our good fortune, she'd shrug it off."

"Anything else?" Marla asked.

"I'd say that was plenty. Wait, there was one other thing. It just came up recently, like within the last two weeks. I was so pumped about getting the new apartment, I shared my good news with him when he popped in. He congratulated me at first, but then his attitude changed when I told him it was rent-free and all I had to do was act as hostess on occasion. He kept pushing to know exactly what my being hostess required. Like I told you, I knew what was going on and planned to get myself out of it somehow down the line, but I played innocent with him. And the more I acted like it was no big deal, the more agitated he got."

"Agitated, in what way?" Rex asked, leaning forward the slightest bit. Chloe probably didn't notice, but Marla did.

"Perhaps that was too strong a description. He didn't warn me off or try to make me see what was actually happening, but he wasn't happy. He pursed his lips and fisted his hands. Shortly after that, he went to see Eloise, but not before he told me to be careful about whatever Eloise asked me to do. I knew what he was saying, but I didn't tell him that. As it turned out, Eloise wasn't in the office at the time, so he stormed off."

She'd just given them some dynamite info. Did she realize what she'd told them?

"What did you make of his actions that day?" Marla asked.

"I had about twelve projects I was trying to finish, so his comments didn't faze me much at the time. But later that night, and especially when I was moving my belongings into the apartment, it struck me how deeply personal he'd gotten. Especially for someone I only knew on a casual basis. Where did he get off disapproving of my life choices?"

"Did you tell him that the next time you saw him?" Rex asked.

"No. I saw him coming and found an excuse to get out of there. At the time, I just acted. But looking back on it now, I can tell my psyche was telling me his interest was inappropriate. Not as a dirty old man but as someone who was taking much too much interest in my personal decisions."

"Anything else you'd like to add?" Marla asked.

Chloe answered immediately without taking time to think about her response. "I'm in my twenties, so I'm supposedly an adult, but I've been without my mother for five years. Although I've been okay financially, it hasn't been easy. My mom was my rock, my conscience. Perhaps there were times when I let Eloise play that role, times when I let her encourage my ambition and baser instincts. I'm not really like that, but I'm not naive, either. I'm just trying to get ahead."

"Bottom-line that for us," Marla told her.

"As much as it may appear that I've benefited from Eloise's death, I didn't kill her."

"Thanks for your time," Rex said, leaving her last comment alone.

Marla couldn't wait before they got away from Chloe and could discuss this last interview, but it was Rex who spoke first once they were back in the SUV. "That was a different Chloe Reardon than the one we met yesterday. She didn't come across so young and naive. But more to the point, she seemed aware of the way she was viewed by the others and didn't apologize for her actions."

"I agree. That actually made her more understandable to me. More human although not necessarily more likeable. But she wasn't going for that. She was going for real, and that we got."

"Let's move on to her visits from Brecken. What did you get from that?"

She had to chuckle. "You want me to go first? Okay, I'm ready. We've wondered about those visits. He could've simply been returning to the familiar despite his relationship with his ex-wife. I get the feeling that even though he's been expanding his business, it may not have been achieving the highs he would've liked, and dropping by the office as frequently as he appears to have done was just to make himself feel better. But we can't discount his interest in Chloe. She was aware of it herself, but she didn't think it was the dirty-old-man kind. We need to take her opinion seriously. But if not of the creepy variety, then what was he after?"

"That's the question of the day. From what I heard Chloe

saying, his questions and comments sounded more like a concerned father. It makes me wish we'd taken my daughter, Cathie, with us. She's an expert on father-daughter relations. She could've told us if Chloe was right to question Brecken's attention or overreactive."

"What about your opinion, Rex?" she asked. "You're a father. Would you have asked questions like that of a young woman you only knew slightly?"

"Maybe as an interviewer but not as an acquaintance."

"So, why? Is he a bit 'off' in that department, or did he have a reason?" she asked.

"What do you think?" he asked her.

"If I was acting as Letitia Carruthers, I'd suspect a twist. Something that was there all along, just not very pronounced."

He stopped the vehicle and pulled over to the curb so he could swivel around to face her. "Okay, let's say you are Letitia Carruthers. What's the twist?"

She cradled her head against the cushioned seat back and forced herself to run everything she knew and had heard about Brecken through her brain at hyper speed and then asked herself to take the leap they suggested. It hit her in a flash. Was this a brainstorm?

"Step on the gas. We've got to get to Goodhue fast before I forget my last thought."

twenty-five

. . .

"Why not share it with me now?" Rex asked as he started the SUV.

"I want you and Goodhue to hear it at the same time. I only want to be laughed at once."

"It's that bad?"

"No. Just a huge leap. If I'm going to take it, I want it to be the three of us together," she replied.

"One for all and all for one? That kind of thing?" he kidded.

"Just drive."

They went to Rex's condo. Goodhue was only a few minutes behind them. Marla and Rex took spots on the sectional and Goodhue chose the easy chair. "Did those financials help?" he asked before Marla had a chance to broach her idea.

"Yeah. But can we put a pin in those for now? Marla's got an idea she wouldn't share with me until you were here, too," Rex said.

Goodhue searched first Rex's eyes then Marla's. "You kids not getting along?"

"It's not that, Chief," Marla said. "Rex and I just finished interviewing Chloe Reardon a second time. Our questions focused on the numerous drop-by visits she received from Brecken Wallace, even after his divorce from Eloise Wallace and even after Eloise became the full owner of Essy."

"What prompted that line?" Goodhue asked.

"It seemed strange to us, his continuing to stop by unexpectedly despite his explaining he just liked to keep in touch with the others that worked there. Plausible, but it just didn't wash with us."

Together, Marla and Rex recounted their interview with Chloe, ending with Brecken's concern about her accepting the deal to act as Eloise's hostess in return for no rent. So much concern, he went to find his ex-wife immediately only to learn she was out of the office.

"Okay, I hear what you've been telling me, but how does it relate to his wife's murder?" Goodhue replied.

"I'll get to that shortly, but bear with us. After our interview with Chloe, Rex and I tried to make some sense of what we'd learned. It was certainly a new Chloe Reardon. One who traded the young and naive act we saw earlier for a sharp, savvy and ambitious persona. But we believed her recollections of what Brecken said and asked on those visits. We both came away with the same impression: He was way out of line for just a casual acquaintance."

"Okay?" Goodhue said.

"At that point, Rex challenged me to go back into Letitia Carruthers mode. As much as it pains me to return there, Letitia was a sharp PI because she always could identify the twist behind her findings. So I gave it a shot." She paused, knowing that her next words could get her thrown off this case, never to investigate for the Maple Knolls police department again. "What if Brecken's unusual interest in Chloe is because he is her father?"

The line of Rex's mouth turned up. Not quite a smile but instead approval.

Goodhue's eyes went wide.

"Too far-fetched?" she asked.

"More like brilliant," Rex replied. "You, not Brecken."

They both turned to Goodhue. "Well, Chief? What do you have to say to that?"

"I'll have to tell Patty Letitia Carruthers isn't dead, even without a script. But even if what you suspect is correct, and I'm not doubting that, that leaves me with at least three questions. How do we prove it, and even if we do, how does it relate to the murder of Eloise Wallace? And most important, how do we prove that?"

She settled back into Rex's sectional. "That's why I wanted to see you simultaneously. We all have to brainstorm those exact questions."

"As for that first question, I say we confront Brecken head-on," Rex said.

"Suppose he denies it," Marla said. "Then what do we do?"

"Continue thinking like Letitia Carruthers and figure out what she would do," Goodhue told her.

That was a cop-out. She'd caught the police chief without anything to offer. But his reference to Letitia stopped Rex from adding his piece. So it was up to her to start. At the risk that this Letitia thing might get out of hand, because she really wanted to keep her alter ego in the past, Marla attempted to answer her own question by channeling Letitia.

"We ask him straight off if he's her father to catch him off guard. Once he denies the relationship, then and only then, we hit him with his concern about Chloe playing hostess for Eloise. We hammer away at the idea of someone who barely knows her coming across so disturbed at the prospect of her possibly prostituting herself. The idea is to shake his self-confidence by continuously turning Chloe's words against him."

Goodhue exchanged a look with Rex. Had she gone too far? She'd given them the best she could come up with when asked to do so on the spot.

"Does she always conceptualize like that?" Goodhue asked Rex.

Rex shot her a conspiratorial look. "Not always, but what you just heard happens frequently. I swear she's stored away some of the story ideas from that show in her subconscious that she pulls up whenever they're needed."

"That's a great approach, Marla, but a lot of it rests on how well you and Rex hit back with your questions. Are you up to it?"

"Rex is," Marla replied, "and I take my cues from him."

Goodhue ran his hand up and down his neck. "I'm with you so far, but where do you go if you can't break him? Rex, it's your turn."

Rex took his time responding. "I'm more into facts and evidence than Marla, who tends to be the people person. So I would've started that way by checking her birth certificate and doing a DNA comparison. I'd also get a warrant to search his home and business for whatever personal data we can find on him. The problem is, my approach would take time, possibly several weeks to get the DNA data, and you want to settle this case quickly."

Goodhue had been nodding throughout Rex's response. "That's pretty much the kind of answer I expected from you, Rex. You're right, you'd be much stronger questioning him about his being her father if you already knew he was. And if the facts didn't support Marla's theory, then we'd have to determine before going in if we should still question his interest in the young woman. But, and this a big but, is it worth investing the time gathering this information?"

The three of them sat there in silence pondering his question.

Marla had hoped for more guidance from Goodhue. Instead, he was putting their next steps back on them.

Her brain sifted through various other alternatives. "Possibly we could learn more about Chloe's late mother by talking to others who might have known her twenty-some years ago when she gave birth to Chloe. The problem with that approach would be getting the initial information from Chloe. Would we want to tip her off that we're looking for her father?"

"Which is exactly why, even though we didn't discuss that approach, we both shied away from it," Rex said to her. "But if we could find someone who knew her mother then, it might take less time than the evidence-gathering I suggested."

"Let's take a step back from this idea that Brecken is her father," Goodhue said. "Would he have had another motive for killing his ex-wife?"

"She treated him like dirt," Marla said. "And he might've thought getting rid of her would get rid of the debt he still owed her. But something would have had to happen to make him snap under those conditions. We haven't uncovered anything like that yet."

"How about the other suspects?" Goodhue asked. "Have you dismissed any of them as the killer?"

"Probably Liz Parsons, our neighbor in the condo building, although we just learned Eloise treated her terribly when they were in college together," Rex replied.

"Nell and Grace both have revenge motives," Marla said. "But why would Grace have waited four years since being forced to sell Essy to Eloise?"

"What about the other woman, the former accountant?" Goodhue asked.

"It's possible," Rex said, "but she's still working through her grief over the death of her late wife. She may not have agreed with some of Eloise's expenditures, but I can't see her killing her, even after being fired."

Goodhue continued going through the list. "And that male assistant? What about him?"

"Tanner's problem was more with Chloe than his boss," Marla replied. "We suspect his negative feelings about her were more from rejection as a lover than from jealousy."

"So, Goodhue," Rex said, "what do you suggest we do?"

"This discussion has been an appreciated exercise on my part, so I feel up to date with the case, but you both already know the answer to that. Go with your gut. I'll get the ball rolling as far as search warrants are concerned for Brecken Wallace's home and business. Keep me posted on the specifics you want included. Keep me posted, period."

twenty-six

. . .

"No wonder that guy was able to climb the administrative ladder," Rex said after seeing Goodhue out of the door of his condo. "That was an amazing tap dance he performed until he left it up to us to decide what we do next. He's now up to speed on our progress while still being able to claim plausible deniability should whatever we decide to do blow up in our face."

Marla could no longer stay seated. "Is that what that was? Every time I expected—needed—guidance, he turned it back on me or you."

He joined her where she had lighted, behind one side of the sectional. "So? What do we want to do?" he asked.

"I want to go for it. Confront Brecken as soon as we can about his paternity. He won't be expecting us to come at him the same day."

He studied her to the point where she wondered if she still had some of her lunch on her face. He took her hands in his. "I take my hat off to your chutzpah. And I'm talking to Marla Dane now, not Letitia Carruthers. That's what I was hoping you'd say.

This could be dangerous if he's our boy and doesn't want to be caught."

She squeezed his hands. "I know. But we survived a killer's wrath once before. We can do it again if it arises."

They texted Goodhue with their decision to move on Brecken Wallace and their intended whereabouts.

They tried to catch Brecken at his house first and, when he wasn't there, went to Grace's instead.

"He's still at work," she told them. "Haven't you asked enough questions for one day?"

"Just a few more," Rex assured her. "I could've asked her not to call ahead and warn him we're on our way," he told Marla once they were back in the SUV, "but that might've raised her alarm."

After they left Grace's house, Marla texted Goodhue that they were headed to Brecken's landscaping business, gave him the address and asked him to meet them there as soon as he and his people could get there.

Wallace Landscaping was located off the main drag in West St. Paul. The front office looked like any ordinary one-story brick office building. The garages and equipment were behind, away from street view. At nearly six in the evening, the front door was already locked, so they made their way around to the back.

Brecken saw them approaching but remained just inside the door of one garage that housed two service vans. The back door of one was open.

"I'll say this for you two. You may not have found my wife's killer yet, but you sure put in long days."

"We think we're close," Rex told him. "But first we have a question for you."

Marla took over from there. "Are you Chloe Reardon's father?"

Brecken took a half a step back but then caught himself. "What a strange question. How does my answering that get you any closer to finding Eloise's killer?"

"Just answer the question, Wallace," Rex said unemotionally.

"No. I don't know what that has to do with anything, but no."

There it was, the denial they didn't want. Twice. Time to apply the screws.

Marla continued. "If that's the case, perhaps you can explain your personal interest in her life, in particular her arrangement with Eloise to stay in the Essy apartment rent-free in return for serving as its hostess."

Brecken shrugged. "Nothing to explain. She's a good kid. I was concerned about what was in her best interest."

"Funny," Rex went on, not backing away from the question, "because she described your interest like that of a father, although she didn't know exactly what that would be like because she'd never known her father."

"I can't speak for Chloe."

"But you tried to, when you bounded off in search of your ex to tell her what you thought of her deal with Chloe," Marla said. "She wasn't there then, but you must've caught up with her later and she laughed in your face. Probably told you it was none of your business and that she had Chloe under her wing if you tried to warn her."

"That's ..."

She didn't let him finish. "Or maybe she already knew you were her father and threatened to tell Chloe if you tried to interfere with their arrangement. As much as you may have wanted to tell Chloe yourself, you've been afraid she'd reject you for not coming forward all these years. That's why you've been attempting to ingratiate yourself with her, helping her become more familiar with you before you told her. But Eloise would have none of it. She wanted to make you pay because you not only left her, but you aligned yourself with her perceived enemy, Grace Adamson. When Eloise refused to budge and bragged about having Chloe under her control, you snapped. You couldn't risk your daughter becoming a carbon copy of Eloise. You had to get rid of her, and what better place to start the process than on her beloved pickleball court?"

"You're blowing smoke, Ms. Dane. You're no longer some PI on TV, so stop trying to be her."

That was his best comeback? To mock her? They had him.

They let her words—pretty good words that no one else had written for her—hang in the air, a silent threat.

"You've said what you came to say. Now leave," Brecken said, still denying their claim.

But Rex wasn't to be swayed. "We've given you the courtesy of telling us yourself, but there are other ways we can make our case. We're already doing a records check. It shouldn't take long to prove your paternity, although that may involve DNA comparisons. Is that how you want Chloe to learn who you really are?"

"You can't make me provide my DNA," a stone-faced Brecken mumbled.

"Actually, we can once we obtain a warrant. That takes a little longer, but we'll see to it that you can't leave town while we wait. And should news that you are our Number One suspect somehow leak, well, we can't control the impact that may have on your clients."

"That's ... that's ... we'll just see what my attorney has to say about your obvious threat."

"Good idea. Have him or her on speed dial to review the search warrants coming your way as we prove you killed your ex-wife. Warrants to search your house, your vehicles and this property for any evidence of poison, duplicate water bottles and any other incriminating items are already underway."

"But all sorts of chemicals are part of my business. You can't use them against me."

Rex turned to Marla. "Pretty good cover, wouldn't you say? Hide behind your business."

With that aside, Rex had thrown it back in her court. But she'd played her best card. Or had she? The strongest reaction they'd gotten from Brecken so far had been his refusal to provide his DNA. Perhaps he was just protecting his individual rights, but on the other hand ...

"Still not ready to reveal your paternity? Perhaps we should start with Chloe instead? Of course, she'll want to know why and ..."

"Shut up! Both of you. Bet you've never been a parent—or discovered you had a child when they were almost grown and were unable to tell them you were their dad because their mother begged you not to stir the waters. The pain is excruciating. It only gets worse when your shrew of a wife finds out and uses it against you."

Maybe that DNA comparison wouldn't be necessary after all.

Before they could follow up on his confession, though, he brought out a handgun he must have had tucked in the back of his pants. "Too bad you're so smart. You've given me no choice." With his gun hand, he gestured to the van next to him, the one with its door already open. "Get in. First, leave your phones here."

A gun. The one thing they hoped wouldn't happen, since they were unarmed. Goodhue and his people would be, but they hadn't arrived yet. They'd have to gut this out. Somehow.

"You don't need to do this, Wallace," said Rex, the former cop trained in talking down killers. "Whatever you plan to do with us will only make the charges worse for you."

"I said to shut up!" Brecken shouted, his face gone as red as Rex's SUV.

Marla fought to restrain her shaking with little success. "This will never unite you with Chloe," she said over the lump in her throat.

"Don't use my daughter as a shield," he cried.

They didn't have any other option, other than to pray Goodhue would arrive soon. Rex climbed in first, then helped Marla up. The vehicle was lined on both sides with shelves full of various cans and boxes filled with landscaping and lawn care products, leaving only a two-foot-wide aisle between them. Thanks to three bags of mulch blocking the aisle, they only had about four feet in which to stand.

Not another close-quarters prison like the last time. Surely he's not going to bind us up with duct tape? They hadn't done so well escaping that one on their own. Now what?

Brecken followed behind but didn't get inside. Instead, he set a can of something just inside the door and ripped off the plug.

The thud of the door slamming shut echoed inside her head.

Rex threw himself against the door, attempting to open it again, but Brecken must have blocked it from the outside.

What was in that can?

The answer became suffocatingly apparent within seconds as the space around them began to mist up. A bug bomb! Lethal insecticide seeped into what was left of the interior space.

They both started coughing, and their eyes began to water.

How much time did they have before they succumbed to the fog? Or died?

Think, Marla! Letitia never faced a fogger. This one was up to her.

They had to stop the outflow, but Brecken had probably taken the plug with him. It probably couldn't be reinserted anyhow. She removed one of her sneakers and covered the top of the can.

The shoe seemed to reduce the flow, but some was still escaping.

Rex pulled a handkerchief from somewhere and covered her face with it.

No time for modesty. She removed her top and stuck it over her head, giving him back his handkerchief. Rex did the same with his own shirt. Both garments would help but not for long.

From what little she could see through the tiny slit in her top, Rex had located a large flowerpot and stuck that over her shoe and the can.

Before she'd covered her face with her top, she'd noted a hoe and shovel along the wall. She'd grabbed the hoe and given Rex the shovel, and they both began banging on the door, praying someone besides Brecken would hear them.

Within minutes, wooziness set in. She tried to remain standing by holding on to the outside wall along the shelf in front of her as she hit the door, but she couldn't fight the overwhelming blackness setting in.

She sank to the floor a couple of seconds ahead of Rex. His body covered most of hers.

The next thing she knew, she came to abruptly when someone kept calling her name.

"Ms. Dane? Can you hear me?"

"Uh ..."

"Don't sit up. Just lie there a bit longer."

A few seconds later, she was whisked away in what must have been an ambulance. She could hear the sirens blaring. Though she didn't pass out, she was only vaguely aware of what was happening. The bug bomb! Someone had come to their rescue. She'd thought she and Rex were goners. Rex? Where was he?

The next few hours passed in a blur, though she remained

conscious. Her lungs and the rest of her body fortunately had not been severely damaged, but the doctors wanted her to stay in the hospital overnight.

"Will you please stop scaring me like that!" Kitty pleaded as soon as she entered the room they'd put her in. "I've only got one sibling, and that's you."

"They ... called ...?"

"Me, of course. I'm your emergency contact. Don't talk. They're still worried about your larynx maybe sustaining damage."

"Bug ..."

"I told you, don't talk. Yes, I've heard a bug bomb nearly did you and Rex in."

"Rex?"

"You are so bad at following orders. Yes, Rex is here also, protesting that he's fine and doesn't need to stay overnight for observation. His daughter, Cathie, is here trying to shut him up just as I'm doing with you. I hope you know you interrupted Hub's pie-baking lesson. He came along with me, delighted to be included in this police business."

"Marla? You really had me scared this time," Chief Goodhue said from the door. "Good thing you texted me all the info. Got there just in time, too. We heard noises coming from one of his vans, but then they stopped suddenly. We got you both out of there as soon as we could."

"Wallace?" she managed to get out, though it hurt her throat.

"Took off, but we caught him on his way to Canada. He's been claiming he hadn't seen you and Rex. And when we accused him of forcing you into his van and setting off a fogger, he swore he had no knowledge of you even being there, that you must have gotten trapped inside the van and inadvertently touched the bug bomb."

Marla tried to shake her head but stopped when it started to throb.

"That's all you need to know for now. You and Rex are safe, and we've got Wallace behind bars. Rest up. We'll talk more tomorrow once the doctors give you the go-ahead." He headed for the door but turned before leaving. "Good job. Both of you."

twenty-seven

. . .

"Are you up for company?" Rex leaned against the door wearing a hospital gown the same as she was.

Though she hadn't been dozing off because her doctor had advised against sleeping, Marla opened her eyes and smiled with relief. "Hi, partner. They assured me you were okay, but I haven't relaxed until seeing you just now."

He made his way slowly into the room, closing the door behind him. "That's why I stumbled down that corridor, my hand holding the back together. Hate for you to see me in this, but I wanted make sure you really survived that trial by bug bomb."

Boy, was she glad to see him! Even in recovery mode, he looked pretty great in that hospital gown. "Barely, but I'm only telling you that," she said. "I hate that we got caught off guard by our suspect again."

"That was my fault. I should've anticipated him having a gun."

"I'm betting Grace warned him we were looking for him, although I don't think she knew what danger that would put us in," she said. "By the way, you look fabulous in that gown."

He chuckled. "Better than the last time you saw me with my shirt over my head. Although that hint of skin you showed when you stripped down to your bra provided its own kind of excitement as I faced death."

"You rogue, you!" She smiled. "Guess I lost my shyness a long time ago after all the fittings I've been subjected to over the years."

"That gesture plus losing your shoe to the can probably saved our lives. So, thanks."

"Did the chief tell you any more about Brecken than he shared with me, which was only that they tracked him down heading north and had him in jail?"

"At that point, he still hadn't confessed. They're holding him on pulling a gun on us, kidnapping and attempted murder. All serious charges, if not murder. Goodhue told me those actions were enough for him to expedite the warrant process. The guy may have been smart enough to get rid of the water bottles and equipment bag, if that's how he got the poison into her, but I'm guessing he thought he could hide the poison amongst all his other chemicals."

"At least our time in that death wagon wasn't in vain."

"Guess I should head back to my room and let you get some needed rest," he said. "By the way, your opening salvo laying out his guilt was brilliant. A hotshot prosecutor couldn't have said it better."

"Thanks. That briefing session earlier with Goodhue helped get my thoughts in order. But it was only after that when you outlined all the ways we planned to nail him that he broke."

"Let's continue our attaboys tomorrow once we're both feeling better," he said. And he was gone.

GOODHUE WAITED until midafternoon the next day to meet with them in Rex's condo. "How are you both feeling today?" he asked first. "I won't minimize how close we came to losing you last night."

"Sorry about that," Rex replied. "I take responsibility. I thought he was ready to come clean. Instead, he pulled that gun."

Marla nodded. "I thought so, too. He'd been so low-key the other times we interviewed him, neither of us anticipated him going all gangster on us."

"That gangster reaction is what will send him to prison," Goodhue said. "Plus, I've saved the best until I was sure you both were okay. Our search of the storeroom at his business netted the discovery of an old can of a herbicide, rich in arsenic. And for some reason, he thought he could hide the duplicate water bottles and equipment bag amongst the items in his attic. We've got him!"

THE DAY AFTER HIS VISIT, Chief Goodhue called Marla and Rex. "I have an unusual request to make of the two of you. Chloe Reardon and Grace Adamson would like to see you. I told them I would allow it only if you both agreed, they each met with the two of you together, and this meeting takes place on my ground, at the station."

"Have they seen Wallace already?" Marla asked.

"Yes. Within the last hour," Goodhue answered.

"Why do they want to see us?" Rex asked.

"I don't know. Each declined to say. They may be bringing you messages from Wallace, or they each may have her own thing to tell you. It's up to you."

"I'm game if Rex is," Marla said.

"We can be there in fifteen minutes," Rex said.

Though Marla was curious to hear what both Grace and Chloe had to say to them, her breathing had almost returned to normal after her life-threatening moments the day before. She wouldn't let whatever they had to say rattle her. Facing death in Wallace's van and surviving it, she felt better than she had in months. Something inside her had changed. She couldn't explain why or how, just that the old Marla Dane was back. No, not the old one. A new Marla. A stronger Marla, especially in spirit.

She shot a sideways glance at Rex to check out how he was reacting to these requests. Typical Rex. Little in his facial expression gave away his thoughts.

"Any idea what we may hear from them?" she asked to break the silence.

"Hopefully they'll have new details to add to those we've already assembled."

"Aren't you the optimist," she replied.

"No sense wasting my mental energy worrying about it until we get there."

Goodhue had set aside a conference room for them to use and had stationed two of his officers at safe distances in the hallway outside as a precaution.

Grace was the first to appear. Marla and Rex sat together across the table from her. Goodhue took a seat at one end.

"I just learned this morning that Breck had been charged with Eloise's murder. I had no clue he was about to be arrested when he and I met with you yesterday. Nor have I ever suspected he was her killer.

"Thank you, Chief Goodhue, for letting me see him, because I had to know why. I thought we were doing fine, even though I no longer owned Essy and he was deep in debt to Eloise.

"When I met with him, he didn't tell me one way or the other if he did it. He's already met with an attorney, who advised him not to say anything further about the case. I didn't ask to speak with you to plead his case nor to exonerate myself. I just want to tell you that despite the fact he may have done this horrible act, the Brecken Wallace I've always known is a good man. At one time he really did love Eloise. I saw that when she first came to work for me.

"But something changed in her over time. And as she changed, so did he. She emasculated him at the same time she betrayed me. If he did indeed murder her, I can understand although not condone it.

"I wanted you two to know that I appreciate the way you treated me throughout your investigation. You were fair and gave me ample opportunity to answer your questions."

"Do either of you want to respond to Ms. Adamson's comments?" Goodhue asked when Grace finished.

"Thank you for your comments," Rex told her. "I'm sure you can understand that we can't say much of anything about a pending case."

She nodded but didn't reply.

"I wish you well," Marla said. She hoped now that both Wallaces were out of her life, providing Brecken was convicted, that Grace would take that money she'd been saving from the sale of Essy and do something new and exciting with it.

Goodhue led her out, leaving Marla and Rex alone to absorb what they just heard.

"What did you get from that discourse?" Rex asked her.

"I'm not sure. I think she was attempting to put distance between herself and Brecken."

A few minutes later, Goodhue ushered a red-eyed Chloe into the room. She took the seat Grace had vacated and focused on her clasped hands in her lap, never once looking at them.

"Okay, Ms. Reardon. You asked to talk to my two investigators, so the table is yours," Goodhue said.

Chloe lifted her eyes and faced Marla and Rex. "I had no idea he was my father. He told me he wanted to be the one to tell me, before the news gets out. He didn't want me to be caught off guard. He also said he'd wanted to tell me many times during the last few years but first had gone along with my mother's wishes not to reveal who he was and more recently because Eloise found out and used it against him.

"There wasn't time to go into everything he wanted to say. He begged me not to judge him too harshly and to give him a chance to be my father, even if it's from prison.

"I hate that I found out this way, but I think I'm happy to finally know. When I was younger, my mother told me my father had died in a car accident. When I was old enough to understand, she told me I was the result of a short affair. She had chosen not to tell the father, and then he had been killed before I was old enough to meet him. It angered me that I hadn't had that chance, but otherwise, she was a wonderful mother.

"Thank you both for making this happen even though it came out of a murder investigation. You must have figured out his relationship to me, but you let him be the one to tell me. I don't know what all convinced you he was the one who murdered Eloise, but if he did, he must have had his reasons. Knowing Eloise, I can understand even though I can't excuse it.

"Despite my new understanding of Eloise, I agreed to follow through on the arrangements he's been making for her. It won't be easy, because it hasn't been that long since I made final arrangements for my mother. But I guess I'm the logical one to finish what he started, since she named me her beneficiary. Plus, he's already taken care of most of it."

"Is that all you wanted to say?" Goodhue asked after she stopped speaking.

"Yes, thank you, Chief. I'm still trying to take in everything I've learned today. I have more questions only my father can answer."

"Ms. Dane, Mr. Alcorn, anything you want to say to Ms. Reardon?" Goodhue asked.

Marla's heart went out to the young woman. Even if she was ambitious and had willingly gone along with Eloise's plans, no one should have to discover the identity of a parent in the midst of a murder investigation. "Have you spoken with Grace since learning about your father?"

"Grace? No. They've kept us separated the whole time we've been here at the station today."

"Although you both appear to be in shock right now, in time, you might want to talk to her," Marla said. Goodhue might not approve of her suggesting the action, but right now, both women needed a friend.

"I'm sorry you had to find out this way," Rex said, "but it couldn't be helped."

Chloe didn't respond but mainly because she seemed to still be absorbing the news.

"Thanks for coming in," Goodhue told them after returning from showing Chloe out. "I would normally say no to such follow-ups, but they both needed to process what they learned this morning."

"Have you completely dismissed Grace as an accomplice?" Rex asked.

"For now. With Brecken not talking at all, there are still a few questions remaining about her part in this, so we'll keep digging. Maybe even obtain a warrant for her place. The county attorney and I will have to bat that one around."

"You don't think that was the purpose behind her wanting to talk to us?" Rex asked. "Don't forget her years spent in her grandparents' pharmacy and her minor in chemistry. She could've been the brains behind administering the arsenic."

"Good point, Alcorn. But for now, my gut tells me she's more hurt than anything else. Not that Brecken spared her knowing any of this but that he was capable of murder in the first place." He turned to Marla. "I'm glad you suggested Ms. Reardon get in touch with Grace Adamson. I couldn't in my official capacity."

"With the funding Grace still has available and with Chloe inheriting Essy from Eloise, there's a chance the two could team up and create something really fabulous, if Chloe is able to shed some of the bad habits she learned from her former boss," Marla said, hoping the two women were smart enough to see that.

"Interesting idea," Rex said, "but since we now have to step back from this case, we'll have to leave it up to them."

THE NEXT DAY, Marla and Rex received a text from Goodhue reporting that following Brecken's visits with Grace and Chloe, Brecken had changed his plea to guilty, indicating both women had assured him they'd support him if he really had killed Eloise. He'd been close to confessing to the crime when Marla and Rex showed up and accused him of the murder. Realizing his chance to come forth on his own was gone, he panicked, forced them into the van at gunpoint and attempted to overcome them with the bug bomb. Having made the situation all the worse with those actions, he followed his attorney's advice to remain silent.

Goodhue and company already had the arsenic and duplicate water bottles to nail him with. But now, after talking to the two women, he supplied the background story, indicating he'd done pretty much as Marla had speculated when they confronted him. A little over six years ago he'd learned from an old acquaintance who knew Chloe's mother and him during that short time they were together that, before he met Eloise, a child had been the result of that liaison. Since then, he'd tried to connect with her. At first, her mother begged him to stay away from her because learning her father had not died in a car accident would only confuse the girl.

He'd told Eloise about the child, thinking it might appease her since she'd lost two babies of her own to miscarriages. Instead, the fact that he had a child and she didn't only added more fuel to the fire of their already deteriorating marriage. She made life miserable for him after that but only agreed to the divorce after he promised not to contact the girl. Then Eloise had made it her business to befriend Chloe on her own, never telling Brecken what she was doing. That was how Eloise became her intern and then was hired onto the staff.

By the time Brecken learned of Eloise's efforts, she and Chloe were already close. That was why he continued to drop by the Essy office when there was no apparent reason for him to be there. He was attempting to get to know Chloe better and protect her from Eloise's mentorship. Then he learned about the setup with the apartment and was frantic to save his daughter from prostituting herself any way he could.

He'd already decided to poison his ex-wife that day by the time Nell confronted her on the pickleball court. He'd gotten the idea weeks back when he'd discovered the old can of herbicide when inventorying his supplies. Though he hadn't orchestrated that blowup, it offered the chance to switch her water bottles with his contaminated ones. Although he'd been reading up on arsenic, evidence of which they found on his personal computer, he hadn't been sure how long it would take to act. He'd played his match, gone home and waited. He hadn't been sure until the police visited him Monday morning that it had worked.

He thought he'd gotten away with it, even after his first interview with Marla and Rex. But then they'd learned about his recent visits to Essy, and he began to fear his free days were numbered.

He didn't apologize for killing Eloise. He was just sorry he'd had to take such drastic steps to protect Chloe.

twenty-eight

. . .

While Marla and Rex were determining who killed Eloise, Kitty and Hub were progressing through his baking lessons.

"You should've seen him," Kitty crowed the day after Marla and Rex had met with Chloe and Grace. "He's a fast study. And he liked it!"

"Any samples available?" Marla asked, suddenly very hungry after several days of eating on the run.

"As a matter of fact, there are two pieces of apple pie in the fridge we saved for you. We tried a cherry pie, too, although since cherries aren't in season, we bought a can of pie filling instead of making it from scratch."

Marla didn't wait to be told a second time where the pie was. While she ate, she texted Rex that a piece was waiting for him if he got there fast enough, before she devoured the second.

"Well? What do you think?" Kitty asked while hanging over her as she tried not to eat too fast.

"This is really quite tasty, Kitty. And flakier than the one we made together."

"I shared Rex's tip about coating the butter before combining it with the flour mixture. It was Hub's idea to add a bit more butter. He's really gotten into this baking thing. He's meeting with his boss today and can't wait to share what he's learned."

Rex joined them a few minutes later.

"Just in time," Marla said. "If I'd had to wait any longer for you to arrive, you might've been out of luck."

Kitty poured him a cup of coffee to accompany his pie. "I met your daughter the other night at the hospital. You hadn't told her you've been consulting for the police. Wish you'd given me a heads-up so I wouldn't have stumbled into telling her what you've been up to."

"Yeah, I got quite an earful while I was supposed to be recovering from my run-in with the bug bomb. And if my latest investigative activities weren't enough to concern her, you'd also mentioned I was working with your sister, Marla Dane, the famous TV star. She threatened to never forgive me for keeping that tidbit from her if I didn't introduce you sometime soon."

"That's great!" Marla said. "After nearly being killed together twice, it's about time I saw the other part of your life."

"Yeah? Why? My life is so low-key compared to yours?"

"You think I'm high-profile just because I was on TV?" Marla replied.

"No, hon," Kitty interrupted. "Because you've got me in your life." And she meant it!

Rex held up his coffee cup for a refill. "Give me a couple days to come down from this case and then we'll figure out a way you can meet my family. Maybe I'll even fix my famous lasagna for you."

"You cook, too?" Kitty said. "You don't just bake pies?"

"You forget, I've been on my own for a number of years. Frozen food, cans and takeout got old after a while."

"I'll look forward to both your cooking and meeting your daughter and the rest of the family," Marla said.

"Me, too," Kitty added. "Oh, looks like I have a text coming in from Hub. I hope things went all right with his boss."

She turned away to read the text. Marla waited for the anticipated shouts and cheers, but they didn't come. Instead, Kitty's shoulders dropped while she continued to face away from them.

"Kitty? Is everything okay? Didn't his boss like his pies?"

Kitty squared her shoulders and turned to face them. "Uh, yes. His boss was quite taken with Hub's demonstration. He offered Hub the promotion on the spot, and Hub immediately accepted."

"That's good news, isn't it?" Rex asked. "Wasn't he hoping for the promotion?"

Kitty pursed her lips. "The new position is in New York City. He never mentioned that part."

"Oh," Marla said, not sure what to say.

"He says his boss was so impressed with his performance that he's talking about Hub doing the commercials in addition to his new job duties."

"That's good, isn't it?" Rex asked. "Isn't that what you've been helping him with and why you pulled Marla and me into the project as well?"

Kitty sniffed, as if she couldn't believe Rex could be so obtuse. "I, uh, thought maybe there was a chance Hub would tell his boss about how much I helped him and his boss would, uh, ask me to do the commercials."

Marla fought the impulse to laugh or to check Rex's expression. She wouldn't dare. This apparently was a big deal to Kitty. "I'm sorry, Kitty. I didn't realize you were seriously hoping for that outcome."

Kitty dropped onto one of the barstools at the kitchen island. "It was just a pipe dream. I didn't really think it would happen. Just something nice to think about." She released a long breath. "There is one positive piece of news, I guess. In return for the help I gave him, he's already suggested my name to Delphine Rambling as a great committee member for her next charity event."

"That's a big deal," Marla said, truly happy for her sister.

"I suppose. But there's another wrinkle. He says since he'll be leaving for New York next week and will be extremely busy packing and arranging for his move, it's best we break things off now. It was great, but yada, yada, yada."

Yet another one bites the dust. Knowing Kitty, she'd pick herself up and find someone new probably before Hub ever got to the Big Apple, but his dumping her had to hurt. "I'm sorry. I know that sounds hollow, but ..."

"Don't waste any pity on me. I knew it wouldn't last, but for him to dump me, and in a text, well, that's a new low for the men I've dated."

"Can we do anything?" Rex asked.

Kitty held her head higher. "Let's not mention pie baking for some time to come!"

twenty-nine

. . .

Kitty escaped to her room to watch TV after first rounding up a tub of cherry-chocolate-nut ice cream, a package of cookies and a can of soda (although she left the Diet Coke for Marla).

"Will she be okay?" Rex asked after Kitty left.

"She's Kitty. She'll be fine in a day or so. Tonight, she needs to lick her wounds."

"Where have I heard that phrase before?" Rex asked, nudging Marla.

She laughed. "Seems to run in the family."

He studied her. "It's good to hear you laugh like that, especially in response to those words."

"I did say them once upon a time, but I don't recall saying them to you."

"No, but I figured as much when I first met you. Reminded me of my favorite pro baseball player when he'd strike out. He didn't throw the bat or argue with the ump but instead took it in stride and held his head high. But in the dugout, he moved off to the end of the bench and sat by himself until he had to take his field position."

"I'm flattered. You just compared me to a baseball player. When not investigating murders, that's your bag."

"It was meant with the greatest respect, because I've seen you begin to slide down your own bench, closer and closer to the rest of the team."

Her breath caught. She was momentarily without words. Rex had just paid her a special compliment, and she didn't know how to respond without insulting him. "What 'field position' have I had to take recently? Was that in reference to my investigating two homicides?"

He stuck his elbows on the island top, templed his hands and planted his chin on top of them. His go-to position when thinking. "I hadn't thought about that part at the time I said it, but yeah, working on those cases has helped you 'slide back down the bench.' Humph, I'm more of a philosopher than I realized."

She reached over and touched his forearm. "That was deep, Rex. You've slid down that bench, too."

He unclasped his hands to take the one she'd placed on his forearm. "Have I impressed you enough with my wisdom to make a suggestion without your rejecting it outright?"

She didn't remove her hand, even after his question. She was intrigued. Rex didn't offer personal advice very often. "Will it hurt?"

"Depends on how far down the bench you've moved. I can see it, but how well can you?"

"I'm feeling better about myself than I have in a long time. Defying death twice seems to have unlocked the old Marla Dane from the self-imposed prison she's been living in. So, yes, I've moved down the bench. Tell me what you have in mind."

"I've been thinking about the problems you said you experienced trying to make a video. Is it possible that once in front of a camera again, you reverted to your on-camera personality, the one that was used to scripts? Since there wasn't one handy, you froze." He paused to let his comment take root and look her straight in the eyes. "Does that come close to what happened?"

Her problems with making a video had been on his mind? That idea was more radical than what he'd asked. But since he'd not only had the thought but also shared it with her, she owed him a candid response.

"A script might've helped, but I think the real problem was that I didn't have a point of view. Yes, my charge was to refresh Kitty's memory of how to bake a pie so she could gain points with her new guy. But how was that helping me make a statement?"

"Good question. Have you answered it in your head?" he asked.

"I'm not there yet. But deciding I need a point of view if I'm to go forward with videocasting was a huge step. I already know it should be about coming back to Minnesota and what that means to me. It means I have to shift from the idea of hiding out to pride in being back home. Somewhere in that notion is my point of view. Being aware of that much, I think I'm ready to do the pie-baking video for Kitty. What do you think?"

He held up the hand that wasn't still holding hers. "Not for me to say. But if you do try, perhaps consider cue cards. Didn't they use those on your show?"

"The regular cast and I had become experts at memorizing new lines each week. But on occasion, guest stars needed a little something to stay on script." Despite that comment, his suggestion had merit. Cue cards might help her stay on point. "Wouldn't I need a full script first to reduce to cue cards?" she asked.

"Not necessarily, although what I had in mind was simply to outline the main thoughts you wanted to get across. For demonstrating how to bake a pie, the cue cards could hit on the main steps, just like the recipe you'd be using."

She considered his suggestion. Using cue cards upped the complexity of the project. All she'd planned to do was get in front of a camera and talk. But look how that had turned out. "On *Carruthers* there was a specific cue card person. There's a certain skill to shifting seamlessly from one card to the next. They usually had to hold ten or twelve cards at a time. Who would I get to do that for me?"

"That's what you're worried about? Sign me up."

Had she heard him correctly? Rex Alcorn, cue card man? "If I were to try doing a video again, I would hope you'd handle the camera. Kitty and Tom have told me you have the equipment."

"Okay, let's not get too specific right now. It's the idea you need to consider trying."

"Don't you want to be my cue card guy?"

"The idea, Marla, the idea. Are you up for trying again?"

"Why are you pushing this?" she asked.

"I don't mean to push." He drew in his lips. "Okay, maybe I do. I think it would be good for you. But I'm just an interested friend. Have you shared the idea with your manager?"

"Jayne Yarmouth, and no, I haven't talked to her for a while. I seem to have been caught up in local murders."

That last part was meant as a joke.

"Maybe you should give her a call, explore the idea of video-casting with her, or are you afraid she'll discourage you because it might not be good for your career?"

"I don't see how raising my profile to the public with a video would be detrimental. But she might have problems with my helping the local police solve murders."

He removed his hand from hers and sat back, narrowing his eyes. "How could catching not one but two killers be perceived as anything but positive? You're a hero, Marla. Goodhue may not be playing it up because he has to make his own department look good, but there's no denying what we've accomplished is pretty great," he said.

He had a point, and to play it down now meant she'd be reducing his part in their recent exploits. Which she didn't want to do. "You're right, Rex. I'm proud of what we've done. But I still need to figure out for myself how investigating two murders plays into the point of view I want in my videocasting."

"Maybe you don't need to answer that question for this particular video. Focus on baking a pie. Do that part for Kitty. Test your chops back in front of a camera again for you. That's all you need to accomplish for now."

"What if there's another murder? Then what?"

"You really think there'd be a third?" he asked. "We've already entered the Twilight Zone of Local Crime with two murders in the same town so close together."

"But if another did occur? Would you still feel obligated to consult?"

"I like having you as my partner, but I don't want to stand in the way of your triumphant return to the entertainment world."

"Was that a yes or a no?"

"It was a 'let's wait and see.' In the meantime, I've got a lasagna dinner to plan and a possible new job producing your video."

"Who said anything about producing?" She laughed.

"I want the title if I'm gonna help you."

"You drive a hard bargain, Rex Alcorn."

"And you wouldn't have it any other way."

epilogue

. . .

$\mathcal{E}$ight months later, having survived her first Minnesota winter in years, Marla stowed her new equipment bag in her service wagon and joined Rex outside the condo building. "How did you talk me into this? I should be home working on my new video now that I've decided my point of view is 'you can go home again.'"

"This is for your video. You said you'd beaten the life out of pie baking, preparing the perfect lasagna and how a Californian adjusts to a Minnesota winter. You wanted to do something new."

"But this? I'm already researching biking and fishing in Minnesota."

"Liz Parsons and the other three want to reassure us they bear no personal grudges against us for treating them as suspects during the Wallace case. Once you said yes, I couldn't very well say no."

"Yes, you could have, and they would've dismissed it as typical Rex Alcorn non-participation in sports, and then I could've ridden your coattails," she replied.

"Look at it this way. You got to buy a new athletic outfit, an equipment bag complete with a beautiful new racket and a fancy water bottle. Plus, Kitty is beside herself that she didn't get invited."

"But I'm out of shape. I stayed with the treadmill routine through the winter but traded that in for walks I didn't take once spring arrived."

"This is just a lesson, not a match. And once today is over, you'll have lots of notes for your video."

They were still debating the pros and cons of this new adventure as they arrived at the Rambling Meadows pickleball court, where they were greeted by Liz, Tanner, Nell, Grace and Chloe. And Scottie?

"You came!" Liz said, bustling over to hug Marla.

"Of course," Marla returned. "We couldn't resist the opportunity to see you all again."

The other five circled them, smiling with excitement.

"I won the bet!" Nell shouted.

"What bet?" Marla asked.

"That both of you would show up," Chloe told them.

"My money was on you, Marla," Liz crowed.

"Sorry, Marla. I was sure you'd find some reason not to be here," Grace said.

"Congratulations, Nell," Rex said. "Did the bet include our staying for the entire lesson, or can we leave now?"

Their six instructors stared back at them dumbfounded until Rex laughed. Heartier than usual.

"Before we get going, tell us how Essy Two is coming along," Marla said to the group.

"Initially, we had some issues to iron out in order to establish Essy Two," Grace said.

"Issues? You're being kind, partner," Chloe said. "When we began to talk about reinventing Essy, the only bond uniting us was the fact that my father and her lover had confessed to murdering her former partner and my boss. Neither one of us trusted the other. I thought she'd been his accomplice, and she thought the same of me."

"They're probably tired of hearing about Eloise's case," Grace said. "We're here today for pickleball, so, Marla, all you two need to know is that eventually we realized we wanted the same thing, for Essy to emerge from the ashes. After I paid for Breck's attorney, I reinvested what was left from selling it to Eloise."

"At Tanner's suggestion, we drew up a compact of under-standing that outlined Grace's responsibilities and mine and detailed the steps we had to take if we ever want to change those details," Chloe said, beaming at Tanner.

"Grace goes back to dreaming up exciting possibilities for new or struggling enterprises, Chloe takes over the business end, I'm assistant to both, and Nell comes back to make sure we're toeing the line financially," Tanner said.

"And then there's me," Liz said, elbowing her way in front of the others. "I'm their great new idea, bringing in my investment expertise in return for their help with my start-up fashion business."

"And your own investment of several thousand dollars," Nell added, joining her.

"Don't forget me," Scottie said. "I'm their public relations specialist-in-training! Part-time for now, to see how I work out, but that's exactly the arrangement I wanted. At my age, I'm a trainee!"

"Impressive," Rex said. "Who'd have thought last fall the five of you would be working together and liking it?"

"We have you to thank for that," Grace said.

"Because we believed your stories and didn't accuse you of Eloise Wallace's death?" Marla asked. They hadn't heard much from any of the five since Brecken had pled guilty and been sentenced to life in prison.

"Well, yes, that," Chloe said, "but more to the point, you suggested Grace and I consider pooling our knowledge and resources."

Grace placed an arm around Chloe's shoulder. "At first, it wasn't easy. I blamed her, and she blamed me for Breck giving in to his fears that she would go over to the dark side if she continued to work with Eloise. He's resigned to spending the rest of his life behind bars. He made me promise I'd look out for her."

"I've visited him on occasion," Chloe said. "We're taking our time getting to know each other. He made me promise the same about Grace. Once we got to talking about how we'd help him survive in prison, your suggestion, Marla, that Grace and I revive the business came back to me. And here we are today."

"Speaking of 'here,' what's the deal about your being back on the pickleball court? None of you seemed to be enjoying the game from what I observed during my one-day stint as water woman," Marla said. "Chloe, you weren't even a member of the team then, and Scottie was the water girl, uh, hydration manager."

The six exchanged collegial looks. "Should we tell her?" Nell asked the others.

"I thought it was our secret pact," Tanner replied.

"But this is Marla," Nell told him. "She was there that day, Eloise's last day on the court. She deserves to hear what's happened since."

"I'm intrigued, guys. What has happened?" Marla asked.

One more shared group look before Nell spoke. "Like we said, those early days of getting Essy Two up and running weren't the most amicable. We all came in with the same petty complaints about each other as before until one day Tanner had

had too much. He called us all together, and after chewing us out in no uncertain terms, suggested we needed to find some activity away from the office to learn to work together."

"Although he's an excellent assistant, he showed great leadership potential in the way he pulled us together," Grace said.

Rex's face screwed up in confusion. "That's great to hear, but where does pickleball come in?"

"Even though winter had already set in ferociously, Tanner found us an indoor court to play on," Grace told them. "At first we just knocked a few balls over the net, but it didn't take long for the four of us to get going. Before we knew it, we were not only enjoying ourselves, we were playing as a team."

"I thought I'd be the fifth wheel until Scottie came on board," Chloe added. "It looked for a while that it would be me against them again, until Tanner noticed. He stopped the game, gave me his racket and showed me how to serve and hit the ball."

"You should have seen the transformation in her," Tanner said proudly. "She was a natural."

"He even bought me my own gear," Chloe said.

"Which she really liked, once I exchanged the green racket for a blue one," Tanner said kiddingly.

Chloe jostled him fondly. "And my shots improved radically once I had the right color."

"Of course, once there were five of us, we had to figure out a way so that everyone got a turn," Liz said. "Tanner, our budding executive, came up with a rotational scheme that allowed each of us to take a breath every so often. Quite the metaphor of our new work arrangement."

"And when Scottie joined Essy Two a few months ago," Liz said, "I paired up with her, which allowed Tanner and Chloe to play together."

"No more water girl for us," Grace said. "We'd all been

bringing our own bottles anyway, so it made more sense to drop that idea and strengthen the team. Besides, the water person was Eloise's idea."

"We plan to give you each an introductory lesson as our way of thanking you for bringing us together," Nell told them.

"Thanks," Rex replied, "but that's not really necessary. We just called it as we saw it."

"But it's good to catch up with you all," Marla said.

"Same for me," Rex added.

Tanner gave the other five some kind of high sign, because Grace, Liz, Nell and Scottie took off for a nearby bench, leaving Chloe and him there as their apparent instructors. He led Rex to the other side of the court. "Do you play tennis, my friend?" Marla heard him say before she got too far into her own lesson.

For someone who had just learned how to play not long before, Chloe was a skillful and patient instructor. As long as she didn't have to move very far, Marla caught on quickly to the underhand serve and the forehand swing. Backhand would come with time and more practice, if she decided to continue.

The lessons lasted twenty minutes. Rex begged off when his back started acting up. Whether that was a real complaint or he took pity on her as she struggled to return the balls Chloe shot to her, Marla wasn't sure. His back hadn't given him any other trouble lately.

"Thanks, guys, that was a lot of fun," Rex told the group that gathered around them as soon as it was clear the lessons were over.

"We appreciate how you went out of your way to share the experience with us," Marla said.

They said their goodbyes and promised to check in with each other occasionally, and then Marla and Rex headed back to the condo building.

"Well?" she asked him once they were out of the others' earshot. "What did you get from that?"

"Honestly? I still prefer golf. How about you?"

"Even though my legs and feet hardly moved, my arms and back will pay for it tomorrow."

"In other words, neither of us is meant for pickleball," he said.

Something made her pause and look back to the courts and their newfound friends. They had already started play. Tanner and Chloe sat on the bench, waiting for their turn.

"I don't think they believed we'd fall in love with the game today," she said. "And even though Chloe and Tanner were great instructors and the lessons were a nice touch, they invited us for another reason."

"You think?"

"Yeah. Actually, they more or less told us what they wanted us to see, but today was to show us."

"That Essy Two is doing fine?" he asked.

"That, but more. It's doing fine because they are doing fine. Last fall they were six individual souls, each hurting in different ways because of Eloise. For better or worse, more for worse because it involved her murder, Eloise is no longer in their lives. In the aftermath, they have come together as a team to run a more productive, successful business. And they couldn't be happier. But that team would never have gelled and gotten off the ground but for one thing."

She gazed fondly back at the courts. "Pickleball."

afterword

Dear Reader,

Thank you for reading this book. If you liked it, won't you please take a minute to leave a review?

To keep up with Marla's new life in Minnesota, sign up for my newsletter at https://www.subscribepage.com/BBCozies.

This is my third cozy mystery series. I've also written seven books in the Nailed It Home Reno Mysteries series and nine books in the Mah Jongg Mystery series. You can learn more about them and also the eleven contemporary romances I've published on my website, www.barbarabarrettbooks.com.

Follow me on Facebook: http://bit.ly/2aXZvG9
Follow me on X: https://twitter.com/bbarrettbooks

excerpt

Curtains for the Condo Casanova

While you wait for Book 3 in the Unscripted Detective Mysteries, check out the first book in the series, *Curtains for the Condo Casanova.*

KITTY LET THE NEXT TWO DAYS PASS without pushing Marla to join her in more of her current activities, sparing her learning the tango at a ballroom dance class and painting a pitcher in Kitty's ceramics class. She hadn't gone far because the community room at Rambling Meadows accommodated a myriad of offerings. Other undertakings like horticulture were offered in the greenhouse and other outbuildings behind the complex owned by the Rambling Family that condo residents were allowed to use.

Marla used Kitty's absences to settle into her room, order out for her special comfort food - seedless white grapes, chips and French onion dip - and schedule a massage at a nearby spa.

The quiet time was a godsend. Many diverse and difficult thoughts had bombarded her lately. To get past licking her wounds, she needed to sort them out and rid herself of as many nonessentials as she could. In a way, the book club encounter had served as a diversion, which she needed right then. But now she had to focus on where she was headed the rest of her life.

She also checked in with both her manager, Jayne Yarmouth, and her agent, Deidre Mansfield. Jayne was the one who'd counseled her to get away from the LA scene for a while. Deidre, who should've been busy finding her new projects the last few months, had conveniently gone AWOL. She probably should be fired, but Marla sensed that's what Deidre wanted, and she didn't plan to give in to her. She half suspected Deidre knew about the producers' plan to replace her long before she knew.

Kitty returned a little after two. "Why are the police here? A van marked Crime Scene Unit, which I saw when I left, is still parked out front. The army of technicians in blue onesies is gone, but they left behind that telltale yellow tape."

"What? Police were on the premises? I had no idea." She hadn't gone near the balcony all day or she might have seen what was happening.

"Sounds like I need to do some reconnaissance around the building," Kitty said, heading for the door. "I'll start next door with Tom Casey."

Her hand barely touched the doorknob when knocking sounded on the other side.

Must be someone who lived in the building; an outsider would've had to ring for entrance.

Marla opened the door, and Scottie rushed in. "They think I did it," she announced dramatically as she flounced around the room. "Me. I'd never hurt a fly."

"Come sit down and tell us what has you so worked up," Marla said, gently guiding the woman to the sofa.

Though she sat, Scottie shook her head back and forth as if

that action would make whatever had happened go away. "It's Drake," she managed to get out, her voice more a cry.

"Drake?" Marla asked, trying to recall if she'd met someone by that name yet.

"Elliot," Scottie mumbled. "Drake Elliot. He's dead."

Learn more at
barbarabarrettbooks.com/curtains-for-the-condo-casanova/

acknowledgments

This book would not have been possible without the input and suggestions of my editor, Chris Kridler, of Sky Diary Productions. Chris also produced the incredible cover, formatted the manuscript and enhanced the back cover blurb.

Thanks also to Sharleen Newton, Harriet Sawyer and Bernadine Marsis for their keen proofing eyes.

As always, thanks to my husband, Veryl, for his ongoing support.

BOOKS BY BARBARA BARRETT

A LITTLE ABOUT
BARBARA BARRETT

Barbara Barrett started reading mysteries when she was pregnant with her first child. When she'd devoured as many Agatha Christies as she could find, she branched out to English village cozies and Ellery Queen. Later, to avoid a midlife crisis, she began writing fiction at night when she wasn't at her day job in human resources for Iowa State Government.

After releasing eleven full-length romance novels and two novellas, she returned to the cozy mystery genre, using one of her retirement pastimes, the game of mah jongg, as her inspiration. Not only has it been a great social outlet, it has also helped keep her mind active when not writing. She has written nine books in her Mah Jongg Mystery cozy series, which features four friends who met each other when playing mah jongg and now find themselves tracking down killers even though they've never received formal investigative training.

Though not an interior designer, that occupation has always fascinated Barbara. Her father was a carpenter and her husband has his own woodworking business. Exposure to their work got her interested in watching numerous home improvement shows on HGTV. Ro and Val, her characters in the seven books in the Nailed It Home Reno Mysteries series, are an amalgam of several HGTV hosts. Barbara used that combination of personality traits for Ro and turned her into a female sleuth who also rehabs older houses.

Her latest cozy mystery series, the Unscripted Detective, features Marla Dane, who played the lead role of private investigator Letitia Carruthers on the TV show, *Carruthers on the Case,* until after six successful seasons she is replaced by a younger actress. When new roles don't come her way, she returns to her home state of Minnesota and camps out in her sister's condo, where she attempts to lick her wounds and rethink her career. If she never hears about another murder, she'll be happy. But try telling that to the locals, even the police chief who asks for her assistance tracking down a killer. *Murder on the Court* is the second book in that series.

Barbara is a member of Sisters in Crime, Sinc-Iowa and Florida Star Fiction Writers.

She is married to the man she met her senior year of college. They have two grown children, eight grandchildren and two great grandchildren.

Now retired, she is a resident of Iowa and also spends time in Minnesota. She earned her B.A. degree in history from the University of Iowa and her master's degree in history from Drake University.

When not in front of her laptop creating her next story, she plays mah jongg, watches TV detective shows and enjoys lunches with friends. Most recently, she has begun to paint in acrylics and is working to evolve her skills.